MAKE-BELIEVE FIANCÉ

MAKE-BELIEVE SERIES

VIVI HOLT

BLACK LAB PRESS

For my Mum

1

Some things, Heath Montgomery understood. He knew about horses, and about ranching, and how to run a business. And he understood poker. Women? Nope. But poker he got.

He leaned forward in his chair and peered over the cards in his hand to survey the three faces staring back at him. The air stank of stale peanuts and sweat. His mouth turned up at one corner. He chuckled silently and drew in a long slow breath as his friends frowned and squinted at their own hands. Finally, he fanned his cards out on the table. "This is it, then."

Adam Gilston, his co-worker and best friend, lay down his hand and rolled his eyes. "You're cruel." He pushed the pile of chips in the middle of the table toward Heath. "Remind me why I ever thought it'd be a good idea to play poker with you?"

Heath laughed and ran his fingers through his hair. "Sorry, dude, I can't help it. I was born to win."

Adam punched him in the shoulder.

"Hey!" complained Heath with a chuckle. "Sore loser."

"Someone's got to bring you back to earth."

"Anyone need another drink?" asked Tim, holding up a pitcher of Coke with ice, his dark eyes gleaming in the dim light.

Heath shook his head. "No thanks, I've had enough. It's just about time to head home. How many hours have we been at this?"

Heath's kid brother Dan groaned and covered a yawn with his fist. "Too many."

"We're getting too old for this," added Adam, blinking reddened eyes as he scooped the cards into a pile.

"But it's tradition," Tim insisted, stacking his chips neatly, his biceps bulging beneath the sleeves of his plain white T-shirt. Every time Tim was around, Heath made a mental note to go to the gym more often. He had a home gymnasium, but preferred the outdoors – riding a horse or roping cattle always seemed preferable to pumping iron.

"Maybe we could come up with a new tradition," Dan offered. He'd always played the peacemaker, even when they were young.

"One that doesn't involve staying awake for an entire weekend to play poker," added Heath, rubbing his tired eyes. He pushed his chips into a drawstring bag and handed it to one of the casino staff standing against the wall. The man, dressed in a black uniform with red trim and a badge that said "RAMON – I'm here to help," took the bag, nodded and headed for the cashier's cage.

"You're all soft," Tim huffed.

Heath laughed. "Old and soft. That sounds about right."

Adam stood and stretched. "Thirty is hardly old."

"It feels a lot older than twenty," said Heath. "We used to be able to stay up all night and keep rolling all day without so much as a single yawn." He missed those days, but at the same time he was glad they were behind him. He liked a quieter life these days – his ranch suited him just fine. He reached for his Stetson and put it on with another yawn. "Let's get some breakfast on the way back. I'm starved." He walked to the door and pushed it open, letting the bright lights of the casino filter into the small dark room.

Ramon returned with the bag, now full of cash. He almost ran into Heath, then took a step back and pulled out a pile of hundred-dollar bills. "Here you go, sir."

"Thank you." Heath stuffed the bills into his jeans pocket as Ramon nodded and hurried off. It was surreal the way the casino always looked the same – day or night, who could tell. Patrons wandered between the tables, drinks in hand, ready to gamble their savings away.

He frowned. There wasn't much about the place that he liked, but he'd put up with the stale air, bright lights and piped-in music for the three men who followed him. He, Tim and Adam had become fast friends at the private high school he'd attended in San Francisco all those years ago, and they met up at least once a year ever since to play poker. His brother Dan joined the group several years ago, tagging along with Heath as he often did.

"Hello, Heath."

The voice to his right made him squeeze his eyes shut for a moment. Then he turned to face the speaker, pasting a smile onto his face. "Chantelle. Fancy seeing you here."

She flicked her long blonde hair over one shoulder and grinned. "I get around."

He resisted the temptation to agree. The last thing he wanted in that moment was to have it out with his ex-girlfriend in the middle of a crowded casino on zero sleep. Instead he nodded and set his hands on his hips. "We're just heading out. Good to see you." He stifled a yawn and managed a farewell smile.

But she stepped in front of him, resting a perfectly manicured hand on his shoulder. "You don't have to go just yet, do you?"

"It's 7 a.m. and we've been up all night," explained Tim, coming up behind him. "We're going to grab some breakfast and hit the hay. And you are?"

"I'm Chantelle. Pleased to meet you." She gave Tim her most dazzling smile.

Heath willed his eyes not to roll. She really knew how to turn on the charm, but after dating her for six months he'd seen that charm was her only asset. Ever since they broke up, he'd done his best to steer clear of her, but she kept showing up like an unlucky penny everywhere he went. It was like she'd pinned a tracking device to him.

Tim smiled knowingly at Heath as he shook Chantelle's hand. "The famous Chantelle. What a pleasure."

Her eyes glinted. "I'm famous now, am I?"

"In our little circle you are," said Adam, kissing her on the cheek. "How are you doing?"

By the time she'd greeted Dan, Heath was itching to get out of there. "Well, good to see you, Chantelle." He spun on his heel and headed for the exit, hoping his entourage came with him.

When he glanced over his shoulder, he saw they were following. But he also saw them smirking and grinning. Great. He knew what they were thinking – why'd he let go of Chantelle Ryan? She was beautiful, charming, accomplished – everything his parents were hoping for in a daughter-in-law.

Which is where she'd set her sights. Never mind that he wasn't in love with her. She didn't care about that – she even told him so. She was happy to get married and wait for the love to come later, she'd said. Just so long as they could be together. That's when he'd known it was over. How could he love someone so shallow, so manipulative, someone who only wanted to be Mrs. Montgomery.

And then she'd laughed at his return to church. She not only refused to join him in his weekly attendance, but her mockery had been like a knife in the gut. How could anyone settle for someone who treated his beliefs like that? He'd rather stay single the rest of his life than marry a woman he wasn't head-over-heels in love with, a woman who'd scorn his faith. And he hadn't found anyone else yet – much to his family's dismay.

The automatic doors slid open and he walked out into the glaring sunlight. His pupils constricted and he held up a hand to shield his eyes, trying to locate the valet parking stand. He saw it to his left and headed toward it, feeling around his pocket for the ticket stub.

Tim bumped his elbow and grinned. "So that's Chantelle, huh? How come you never mentioned she was so hot?"

"Eh, I guess she is." Heath wasn't in the mood to talk about his ex.

"You guess?" exclaimed Tim, with a whistle. "I can't imagine how high your standards must be if you think she's mediocre."

Heath shrugged and rubbed his eyes as they waited for the parking attendant to retrieve their vehicles. "I know she's pretty. But when you get to know her ..."

"Oh, I'd love to," said Tim with a chuckle and a backward glance.

Heath's eyebrows arched.

"Don't worry, bro, I know the code – I won't date your ex. No matter how hot she might be." He sighed and held a hand to his heart as though it were broken.

Heath laughed. "In this case, I'd say you're welcome to her. But I don't think you'd be happy."

Tim frowned. "Oh?"

"She's only interested in a thick wallet, if you get my drift." Heath shook his head. It had taken him longer than it should've to figure that out. But once he had – and once she'd aired her views on his beliefs – he'd parted ways with her and hadn't looked back.

Tim nodded, his short brown hair shining in the bright morning sunlight and his blue eyes twinkling. "Ah, I get it. Only *in it to win it*, then. Shame ..."

"It's not like you don't have your pick of women

throwing themselves at you, *Fireman Tim*." Heath grinned.

Tim laughed. "It's not like that – trust me. Anyway, none have really caught my eye yet."

"Yeah, me neither."

"So what type of woman are you looking for?" asked Tim.

"Someone real and genuine, fun, down to earth ... I don't know. Just someone who isn't impressed by my name, but who really *sees* me. You know?"

Tim, Adam and Dan looked at him as though he'd lost his mind. "And where do you think you'll find someone like that?" asked Adam, one eyebrow raised high.

"That's the question," said Heath. "Probably not in a place like this." He nodded toward the casino.

"You might be right about that," replied Tim with a chuckle.

A beat-up blue truck rumbled into the space in front of them. The attendant jumped out, jogged around the front of the truck and up to Heath. "Here you go, Mr. Montgomery," he said with a smile.

Heath handed him a tip. "Thanks."

"Why do you keep this old thing?" asked Tim as he climbed in the passenger side.

Heath sat in the driver's seat and shut the door behind him. He sighed and relaxed against the uphol-stery, glad to be back behind the wheel. It felt like home. "Because I like it. It's comfortable."

"You could afford to buy every truck on the lot," replied Tim with a chuckle.

"So what? Shiny things don't impress me. I want something that feels right, that I know I can depend on." Heath pressed on the accelerator and glanced into his rearview mirror to see Adam's car following them with Dan in the passenger seat. He pulled out onto the main road, his mind wandering over everything they'd discussed.

His own words rang in his ears – is that what was missing? He'd dated plenty of women through his twenties, but none had ever felt quite right. Since Chantelle, he'd sworn off dating – he was sick of the awkwardness, the games, and how it never resulted in anything but heartache. He was older now, and knew what he wanted. Someone genuine, a woman he could depend on, who was loyal and loving and real.

Heath sighed as he remembered Adam's words. Where would he find a woman like that?

~

HEATH TURNED the truck into the *Lucky Diner* lot and shut off the engine. "Does this place look okay?" he asked.

Tim nodded and licked his lips. "It looks fine to me. I could eat a horse and chase the rider, I'm so hungry."

Heath chuckled. "Where on Earth did you pick up that saying?"

"In Australia. I was there last year running a collaborative training program for disaster preparedness."

Heath arched an eyebrow. "You really do live a crazy life, you know that?"

Tim shrugged. "I guess. I'm traveling more than

I'd like to – staying in hotels, eating in restaurants, meeting different people everywhere ..."

"My heart bleeds," replied Heath with a laugh.

Tim chuckled. "Okay, I do love it. But lately it's been a bit lonely."

"I guess I can understand that."

They climbed out of the truck just as Adam's Prius pulled up beside them. The two tall, strapping men climbed out, Dan unfolding his limbs with a groan. "Did you buy the smallest car you could find?" he grumbled. Adam lunged for him, but Dan danced out of the way.

Heath smiled. Those two were always going at it, trying to one-up each other. They'd been that way even in high school, both so competitive, neither willing to give in. Even though Dan was two years younger, he'd always tried to keep up with the older group of friends.

"It's good for the environment," Adam growled as the foursome marched into the diner. "Anyway, my wife picked it out."

A bell rang over the door. Heath glanced up at it and his eyes narrowed. A sprig of mistletoe hung beside the bell. It was July.

The smell of fried potatoes mingled with apple pie and coffee distracted him from the incongruous greenery. He stopped, wondering if they should seat themselves or wait to be seated. After a few moments, when no one came to assist them, he led the group to an empty booth against a window at the far end of the diner. Adam and Dan were still rough-housing. He glared at them, slid in beside Dan and quietly dug an elbow into his brother's side.

The waitress walked over, tugged a pencil from behind her ear and held up a pad of paper, barely looking up as she asked for their order. Heath studied her with a half-smile. There was something about her that intrigued him. She was beautiful, but not in an obvious way. She wore no makeup, her blonde hair was pulled back into a tight ponytail and dark circles lined her eyes – it made her seem almost plain at first glance.

The other men gave their orders. Finally, it was Heath's turn. She glanced up at him, then back at the pad. He smiled, watching her closely. She looked tired. Not that he knew what she usually looked like, but she seemed a couple of years younger than him and those dark circles couldn't be there for any other reason. He wished he could ask her about it. "What do you recommend?" he asked.

She arched an eyebrow and chewed on the end of her pencil before answering. "Um ... the waffles are good."

He nodded. "Waffles then, please, and two eggs over easy."

"Coffee?"

"Yes, please, with cream."

With a curt nod and brief smile, she turned and headed for the kitchen.

Heath pushed himself out of the booth and jogged after her. "Excuse me?"

She faced him with a startled frown. "Yes?"

"I'm sorry. I noticed you're not wearing a name tag – just wondering what we should call you, since you're our server and all."

One eyebrow arched. "Gwen. You can call me Gwen."

"I'm Heath. Pleased to meet you, Gwen ... is that short for something?"

Her eyes narrowed. "No."

He chuckled. He seemed to be striking out at every turn. She wasn't interested in a conversation or anything else with him, that much was clear.

His phone buzzed in his pocket. He yanked it out to see who was calling at such an early hour. He swiped his finger across the screen, nodding an apology to Gwen. She pasted a smile on her face and walked away. "Dad. How can I help you?"

"Where are you?" Graham Montgomery's voice boomed down the phone line.

"I'm having breakfast."

"It's almost eight o'clock and there's a senior leadership meeting at the office in ten minutes."

Heath slapped his forehead. "Sorry, Dad – it's my annual weekend with the guys from school. Dan's with us too. We're just having breakfast before heading home." Silence on the other end of the line. "Hello? Dad?"

"So what have you been up to all weekend? All kinds of debauchery, no doubt."

Heath frowned and shook his head. "No, Dad, we just played poker at Montana Nugget, and before that we were out at the ranch. I'm heading back to the ranch now and can be in the office within an hour or so. What's the meeting about?"

"Forget it. Finish your breakfast."

"Come on, Dad ..."

"No. I'll take care of it this time, son. But let me

ask you ... when are you going to take yourself seriously?"

"Dad ..."

"I mean it. It's time for you to settle down, son. You're not twenty anymore."

"I know that, Dad." Heath took a quick breath. It was always the same thing. "I know I gave you trouble when I was younger, but like you said, I'm not a kid anymore. I work hard every single day, Dad. You know that. I've earned a weekend off."

"You should be married by now. At your age, I had two children and was running my own ranch."

His eyes closed and he frowned. "I know."

"It's time to take responsibility, son. Responsibility for your life, for the company ... you can't live this way forever. These weekends with the boys are just another symptom of you trying to hold onto your childhood. But you're not a child any longer – you're a man. It's time you started acting like one."

A hint of sarcasm crept into his voice. "And what does that mean, Dad, to act like a man?"

"It means... well, who are you bringing to your cousin's wedding?"

"What?"

"The wedding this weekend. Who are you bring-ing? You do have a date, don't you?"

Heath bit his lip. Not only didn't he have a date for the wedding, but he'd forgotten all about the event. "Of course I do – I'll tell you all about her soon. But right now I have to go."

His father grunted into the phone. "Well, that's good to hear. You're not getting any younger, you know? I want to give you the CEO position and take a step back, son, but I'm still not convinced you're ready. If you could show me you're growing up ... well, maybe we could finally take that trip I've been promising your mother."

"I hear you, Dad – I just don't agree. I *have* matured. I've been busting my tail running the company and we're bringing in higher profits than ever before. We've added four ranches to our portfolio in the past twelve months, along with half a dozen feed and produce stores, and we'll be expanding into more stores in other states next year. Business is good and it's getting better. That should be all you need to know to make your decision. And if you can't see that, I don't know what to tell you."

Graham seemed to sense he'd crossed a line. "Now, son ..."

But now Heath was boiling. His father had a way of bringing out that side of him and he didn't like it, yet couldn't seem to stop it. "Since you insist on nosing into my private life, I'll be sure to keep you updated on my relationship status from now on. If you like, I can even get Social Security numbers so you can run background checks."

His father sighed. "I know you're doing well, Heath. I keep up with what you're doing at work. I just have some concerns. I want you to be settled, happy. And I'm looking forward to meeting this mystery date of yours."

"She's no mystery, Dad. Look, I have to go – I'm being rude to the guys, and our food is on the table."

His father rang off with a promise to let him know how things went in the meeting. And Heath wandered back to the booth to find Gwen setting plates on the table. He slid into his seat, the aroma of freshly-made waffles with maple syrup and butter drifting up to greet him. His stomach growled and he smiled at Gwen.

She returned his smile half-heartedly as she finished delivering the meals. "I'll be back with your coffee – let me know if you need anything else," she said, wiping her hands on the apron tied neatly about her trim waist.

He watched her leave, then sliced off a piece of waffle. As he put it in his mouth, Tim glanced up at him from his stack of pancakes. "Who was that on the phone?"

"Dad."

"You didn't look real happy about whatever he was saying," Dan added between mouthfuls of egg.

Heath chewed, swallowed and cut another piece. "Yeah. You know the usual – when are you gonna get married, settle down and grow up?" He was tired of hearing about it, from both parents. According to his mother, thirty was far too old to be a respectable bachelor; according to his father, it showed he wasn't sensible enough to run the company. Never mind that he'd basically been managing it for two years already, since his father's heart attack slowed him down.

For some reason, they were both so invested in the idea of him marrying and having a family, they couldn't swallow the idea that perhaps he was the man they wanted him to become already, just single. And they never gave him a break about it, let alone the benefit of the doubt.

Dan chuckled. "I've heard that speech before. So what are you gonna do?"

"Find a date for our cousin's wedding this weekend. Seeing as I already told him I had one, just to get him off my back."

"I get that. Who do you have in mind?"

Heath shook his head. "No one. But I'd better fix that, and fast."

2

GWEN ALDER DUCKED HER HEAD AND WIPED THE SWEAT off her forehead. She still wasn't accustomed to Montana weather. After living most of her life in southern California, she'd moved to the northern Rockies five years earlier when her husband was offered a job there, and shivered through five Arctic winters. Spring wasn't much better, to her way of thinking – the snow finally melted in the low country, but the distant mountain peaks were white against the blue sky, and the winds carried their chill through the city streets.

And now summer, which in Montana was nothing like SoCal. No dry heat and cool oceans here, and nowhere she could escape the humidity. At the diner, the sizzling grill and constant stream of customers meant the thermometer rarely dipped below eighty-five. At her apartment, the air-conditioning unit clunked and clamored for a half-hour each night when she returned home before giving up entirely, leaving her panting and sweating on top of the bedsheets.

She ran a hand over her face, then wiped the sweat on her pants leg. With a grimace she looked at her hand and saw chipped nails and dry skin. When had she stopped taking care of herself? Probably after the first couple years of marriage, when she'd realized it wasn't going to work out. That was when everything had begun to unravel.

Though if she was being completely honest, she'd known from day one the marriage wouldn't last. It wasn't that Edward was mean, at least not at first. But the moment they said "I do," he changed. Gone was the romance, the charm and the thoughtfulness – instead, he was lazy, short-tempered and demanding. When he lost his job in Missoula, she'd found herself supporting them both on her teacher's salary.

Well, all that was behind her now – or most of it. When he left her for a woman from the local dry cleaner, he'd used what money they had left to hire a top-notch attorney who took *her* to the cleaners during the divorce settlement. She'd had to settle for Fran Hall, a well-meaning if scatterbrained ambu-lance-chaser she'd found in a Google search. She shook her head and took a long breath. She'd defi-nitely think twice before marrying again.

Her thoughts turned to her upcoming job at Houghton Elementary School in Billings in two weeks. Butterflies jostled in her stomach. It was nerve-wracking to begin again somewhere new, but she'd already come so far. She'd applied for and accepted a good position, found an apartment to rent (granted, a tiny, sparsely-furnished studio in a bad part of town, but still), and nabbed a summer job waitressing at a local diner to pay the bills until school started at the end of August. Things were finally looking up. Now if only she could get on top of all those bills ...

Her phone rang and she pulled it from her pocket, almost dropping it on the pavement in her haste. Her heart lurched and she paled. The last thing she needed was another expense.

When she answered, her heart seized again. "Gwen!" Fran always sounded like she was shouting out a drill command. It would be funny if it weren't for the dread that curled like a snake in the pit of Gwen's stomach at the sound.

"Hello, Fran. How can I help you?"

"I've got bad news!"

Fran never seemed to have any other kind. "What now? The divorce was finalized last week – what else can he expect from me?"

Fran cackled, her version of a laugh. "Edward's lawyer is complaining about the money they were due to receive from the sale of the house."

"Like that's somehow my fault? Yeah, it isn't as much as we'd hoped, but there's nothing I can do about the housing market. And I have no control over when they receive their half – that's up to the bank." She ran a hand over her face and tried to calm her racing heart. Even hearing Ed's name these days made her break out in a cold sweat.

"He's saying you're holding back!"

"I don't know what to tell you. We got fifty percent of the equity each after legal fees and taxes – which amounted to almost nothing. They know this – they've got a copy of the closing documents." Isn't that what she was paying Fran to handle? She shook her head. She'd been disappointed herself when she saw the figures, but disappointment had become a way of life for her by then.

It was only when she received the job offer from Billings Public Schools that she began to hope again, that perhaps she could change the course of her life. Getting away, starting over – she just wanted some time alone to gather herself, to find the person inside she'd lost sight of over those few years of marriage to Ed.

"Now they're threatening to go back to court and seek alimony!"

Gwen laughed, almost hysterically. "Alimony? I'm working as a waitress at a greasy spoon – I'm basically living off tips, since the hourly wage is practically nothing."

"Yes, but he knows you start teaching in a couple of weeks!"

She frowned, her nostrils flaring in anger. "So that's his plan? He's going to wait until I start teaching and what, garnish my wages? When does it all end, Fran?"

Fran cleared her throat and she heard the rustle of papers down the line. When she spoke again, the drill-sergeant tone was gone. "I'm sorry, Gwen. I know the settlement wasn't what you'd hoped for ..."

"No, it wasn't, and I know there's nothing I can do about that. But something has to change. With taxes and moving costs and your fees, I can't even afford to pay my rent. I'm just hoping my landlord gives me some time to make it up."

"Look, I'm sure it will all resolve itself when

Edward finds work. But right now, he needs support, and ..."

"No! No, he does not 'need support' – and he certainly doesn't need mine! He needs to figure his life out. We're not married anymore ..." Gwen sighed and squeezed her eyes shut. She stopped walking and leaned against a brick wall, enjoying the coolness against her skin. "It feels like I'll never be free."

Fran coughed. "Look, keep your chin up. You'll get through this."

"Thanks, Fran. Don't give him anything, okay?" She wrapped up the call, then groaned against the bricks. So much for starting over. She rubbed her eyes as her throat tightened, the telltale sign of tears. She coughed and bit her lip. There was no time for tears now, not out in the street with people watching. She'd cry later into her pillow.

She smiled – it was almost humorous the way her life was falling to ruin. A giggle rose in her chest. She'd better get inside before she completely lost it in public.

As she jogged toward the apartment, her thoughts returned to the group of men who'd come into the diner that morning. They looked like they'd been up all night, disheveled with three-day beards and wrinkled clothes. Partiers, no doubt – either out drinking or enjoying one of the many local casinos.

It was a shame, because one of them, the one who'd introduced himself as Heath, was cute. Handsome, really. He didn't look much older than her, and had come into the diner sporting a Stetson. There were plenty of cowboys moseying around Billings, and she had a soft spot for them – or had, until Ed had torn her heart out and filleted it. Now, she intended to steer clear of all men until her wounded heart fully healed.

Anyway, she'd known men like Heath before – confident, self-assured and good-looking. No doubt he had women throwing themselves at him all the time. He wouldn't look twice at her.

The apartment building where she lived loomed dark on the next block, its chipped bricks stained with clinging black mold. She pushed through the front door and it swung shut behind her, catching her heel. She glanced over her shoulder as the door slapped her backside and frowned. What was that on the grassy verge outside? It looked like her silver-and-blue bed cover ...

She spun around and jogged to the curb, her heart in her throat. Everything she owned lay on the grass: her bedcovers, the small TV/DVD combo she'd bought at Wal-Mart years earlier, the few books she hadn't donated before the move. It was all there in a pile on the side of the road. Her throat constricted and bile rose from her stomach. What was going on? She knew she was behind on rent, but she'd spoken to the landlord and thought he'd agreed to give her time to make up the payments.

Back inside, she sprinted up the stairs two at a time until she was gasping for breath. She reached her apartment door on the third floor and leaned against the wall as she gulped air. Stars danced before her eyes – she really should exercise more often.

Her key didn't work in the lock and she groaned. There was a piece of pale blue paper taped to the door. An eviction notice.

She sighed and slid down to kneel on the floor, her head in her hands. Tears threatened and she swallowed them down. She had to think. Where could she go now? Her few possessions were out on the curb – she had to get them before someone else did.

Struggling to her feet, she hurried down the staircase again to her old Toyota Corolla, still parked in her assigned space. She climbed in, drove it to the curb and piled everything she could into the trunk and back seats. Good thing the apartment had come furnished, albeit cheaply – she would've had to leave any furniture behind.

Once she was done, she pulled away from the curb and headed through downtown Billings. What next? She had nowhere to go – she was officially homeless. Again the hysterical laughter rose, and this time she let it loose. She laughed until tears rolled down her face and the guffaws morphed into sobs she couldn't contain. When they ran out, she took a deep breath. No point in wallowing – she'd think of something to do.

But for now, she would take a moment and have a coffee. She'd been on her feet all day, the sun was beginning to set, and soon she'd have to make a decision about where she'd spend the night. Her stomach growled and her head felt light. She needed sustenance before she could think clearly enough to make that kind of decision.

She pulled into a parking lot behind the local café, the Cat's Meow, and went inside. It was a quiet time of day, between the dinner and late-night rushes, and one of the two staff on duty was mopping the floor at the far end of the room. She took a seat close to the cash register, ordered, then pulled out her phone. Who could she call?

Out of ideas, she set it on the table as a waitress bought her coffee. "Had a good day?" she asked with a warm smile.

Gwen winced. "I've had better. But thanks for asking."

"Oh?"

"Yeah. I have to find a place to stay."

"Sorry to hear that. You should check the notice board by the front door. There're usually a few rooms for rent and stuff like that posted." The woman wandered behind the register, where she began wiping down the counter.

Gwen's eyes narrowed. She took a sip of coffee, then headed for the notice board. It was a corkboard tacked to the wall, covered in flyers of all shapes and sizes. She scanned the papers, her eyes finally landing on one from a man looking for a roommate. Nope. Another was for a commune on the outskirts of town. No, thank you!

Then a light blue flyer caught her eye. In small type it explained that a single young woman was looking for a roommate to share an apartment near downtown. It looked new – perhaps no one had claimed the room yet. She dialed the number and listened as it rang.

"Hello, this is Diana."

"Diana, my name is Gwen Alder. I'm at the Cat's Meow Café and saw your ad for a roommate. I'm looking for a place and I thought I'd call and ask if yours is still available." Her mind raced over the possibilities, which seemed slim. There wasn't much chance Diana would skip over the credit check, and if they got to that stage she'd soon see why Gwen was homeless.

"Yes, the room's still open."

"Can I come and take a look at it?" asked Gwen, her heart in her throat.

"Sure, that would be fine. When would you like to do that?"

"How about now?"

There was a pause. "Now?"

"Yes, please. I have some time free and I'd really like to move quickly."

"Umm ... okay, now would be fine. I haven't had a chance to clean up ..."

Gwen grinned. "Don't worry about that. I'm sure it'll be lovely."

Diana gave Gwen directions and they ended the call. Gwen sent up a silent prayer of thanks, headed back to her table, gulped down her coffee, paid, collected her purse and walked to her car. All she could do was hope Diana would let her stay. Otherwise, she would be sleeping in the Corolla tonight.

The apartment was in a small complex of eight, neatly maintained if a little cramped. Still, it was all Gwen could do to keep her excitement contained while Diana showed her around. "... And this would be your room." Diana pushed open a door to reveal a small, clean room with gray carpet and worn paint. She chewed on a red painted fingernail, her dark bob falling over wide brown eyes. She shoved it behind her ears with both hands, then resumed worrying her nail.

"It's perfect," said Gwen with a smile. "How soon

could I move in? That is, if you've made your decision."

Diana's eyebrows arched high. "I guess as soon as possible. I really need help with the rent and the room's empty, so ..."

"How about now?" Gwen knew she was pushing it, but didn't have a choice.

Diana laughed. "Now? Well, you're raring to go, aren't you? There are just a couple of things I'll need."

"Of course – shoot."

"A month's rent in advance and a letter of recommendation. I'm sure you understand ..."

"I do understand – that makes sense. It's just that ... it might take me a few days to get those things, and I'd really like to move my things in now. They're down in my car."

Diana frowned. "I see. Have you just arrived in town?"

"Not long ago. And I was staying somewhere, but that fell through today. I'm starting a teaching job in two weeks and waitressing at the Lucky Diner until then, so I'll be able to cover rent. I just need some time."

"Hmmm ... okay, I guess I can deal with that. If you can get me the first month and letter of recommendation by the end of the weekend, you can move in now. I'm taking a risk trusting you, but I usually have pretty good instincts about people and I can tell you're a decent person." Diana grinned and crossed her arms.

Gwen almost cried out in relief. "Thank you, Diana, thank you so much. You're a real lifesaver. I mean it." She threw her arms around Diana, almost knocking her off her feet.

Diana's eyes widened and she patted Gwen's back. "No problem. Happy to help."

Gwen's phone buzzed in her purse and she released Diana to retrieve it. "Sorry."

Diana shook her head. "Sure. I've got to go study. Here are your keys and welcome." She turned and disappeared into her bedroom, closing the door behind her.

Gwen peered at the screen of her phone. Edward. She dropped it back into her purse and squeezed her eyes shut. She didn't want to talk to him. Not now, not ever if she could help it. She wished she could've hired a better lawyer.

Gwen set her purse on the kitchen counter and left the apartment to get her things from the car. At least her new apartment was only on the first floor. She was grateful for small mercies.

3

THE RANCH HOUSE SEEMED QUIET WHEN HEATH WOKE Tuesday morning. After a weekend of having four men there watching baseball, playing cards or swimming in the pool, it seemed empty. He'd taken Tim to the airport the previous evening and collapsed in bed early. Adam and Dan lived in town, and Adam had driven Dan home after Heath and Tim left for the airport.

After a good ten hours' sleep, he felt better than he had in months. He couldn't remember the last time he'd had a day off work. Perhaps in April when he'd taken Chantelle for a picnic – and she'd complained the entire time about the mosquitoes and the mud on her six-inch platform heels. Never mind that he'd told her ahead of time to dress for the outdoors. He rolled his eyes at the memory of her picking her way through the field, disdain pinching her pretty face.

He pulled his truck into the parking garage beneath the twelve-story Montgomery Ranches corporate headquarters. The elevator ride to the top was quiet, as employees greeted him with silent nods or brief good mornings. It was part of the job he'd come to expect. Being the boss meant that people were reluctant to speak to or share much with him. It'd been hard at first, but he was used to it now. It was intimidating holding a conversation with the boss. Even for him, since the boss happened to be his father.

When he reached the twelfth floor, he headed down the hall to his corner office. The office next to his was Adam's. Adam, in addition to being Montgomery Ranches' chief financial officer, was his only married friend, a fact his father liked to point out as often as possible. Adam stepped into the hall with a sheaf of papers in his hands just as Heath walked by. "Heath, there you are."

Heath nodded. "Morning, Adam. Did they survive without us here yesterday?" He chuckled, knowing full well the place would run like clockwork whether they were there or not. It was the way he liked things to be, and he'd purposely set it up to function seamlessly so he could focus on the most important issues.

"Only just." Adam grinned. "Of course, Judy had no one to eat lunch with."

"Where is she?" Adam's wife was also their shared personal assistant. Their romance had been something of a scandal five years earlier, though the outrage had died down as soon as they married.

"I might as well tell you, since you'll be hearing soon enough ... morning sickness," said Adam proudly.

Heath's eyes widened and he laughed out loud.

"Really? Oh man, that's great. Congratulations!" He embraced Adam and pounded his friend on the back.

Adam returned the hug, then stepped back with a smile. "Thanks, man. I'm sorry I didn't say anything over the weekend, but she didn't want me to just yet. We're really excited – cautious, but excited."

"You've been trying for how long now, four years?"

"Yep. Four long years of IVF and healthy eating and wondering and waiting ... and finally she's expecting. We're through the first trimester, so we told the family last night. She wants to wait to tell everyone else officially at work, but I thought you should know."

"I'm so happy for both of you. That's really brightened my day." Heath's heart soared. He knew how much they'd longed for that positive pregnancy test, how many tears had been shed over the possibility it might never happen.

"Lunch?" asked Adam, moving off down the hall.

"Yes, definitely," replied Heath. He prayed a prayer of thanks, then walked to his desk, the grin still on his face. He was so happy for them. He knew that's what his parents wanted for him – they only wanted him to be happy. But maybe it wasn't in the cards for him, and he'd be fine with a single life. Wouldn't he?

ADAM STOOD by the elevator and waved to Heath as he walked toward him. "Ready?" he asked.

Heath nodded. "I didn't think that last meeting would ever end," he complained. He ran a hand over his eyes and squeezed them tightly shut as the elevator whirred toward their floor.

"The board meeting?"

"Yes. It was the longest we've had in months. There was a lot to discuss, decisions to make. And everyone has their opinion about what we should do. Plus, I think they all hate me." He shrugged and sighed. "I felt as though I was being held hostage. And I'm starved."

"Where do you want to eat?"

An image of a blonde waitress flashed before his eyes. "How about the Lucky Diner over on Third?"

The elevator doors swished open and they crammed themselves into the small space left between a dozen other suited staff on their way down. "The Lucky Diner?" questioned Adam with a frown. "Where we ate breakfast yesterday?"

"I know, it's not exactly fine dining," replied Heath. "But ..."

"Fine with me ... I'm sick of all the frou-frou food around here. I could use a good cheesesteak." Adam laughed and patted his lean stomach. "Especially after all the kale smoothies and almond bliss balls my wife's been making me eat."

Heath chuckled. "Cheesesteak it is."

The cheesesteak sandwich was as good as the waffles had been. Rich, moist and flavorful, it filled Heath's growling stomach and made him a little queasy all at the same time, as all good diner food did.

"So is that all you're worried about? Because you seem tense." Adam could always tell when he was out of sorts.

"The board? Yeah, I guess so."

"Don't sweat them much. They're not losing confidence in you, they're just being thorough. Your dad has had the same board for almost twenty years now with one or two exceptions. They just don't like change." Adam took a bite of his sandwich and dabbed his chin with a napkin.

"Yeah, you're probably right. I'm just stressed. Dad's supposed to be announcing anytime now that I'll be taking over as CEO, and I don't want any missteps to make people think I'm not up for the job. I know some of the staff have misgivings ..."

"That was years ago. You've grown since then. You're the right person for the job and everyone can see that now."

Heath grimaced and set his sandwich down on the plate. "I hope you're right. Sometimes I don't feel up to it."

"You've been acting CEO for two years, Heath. There won't be any surprises. You'll be great."

Adam was always cheering him on. It felt good to have a friend like that. Especially when his own parents not only echoed his own internal doubts, but amplified them. "Thanks, Adam, I appreciate your support. You always know what to say to make me feel better."

He glanced around the diner. He'd seen Gwen when they came in, but she'd soon disappeared and they'd been served by another waitress. Since then, he'd only glimpsed her rushing by at various times, busy with the lunch crowd. She looked even more fatigued today than yesterday, if that was possible. He noticed she wasn't wearing a wedding band, but other than possibly being single he didn't know anything else about her. There were so many things he wanted to ask her, but he wasn't sure how.

Heath smiled and wiped his mouth with the napkin from his lap, then settled back in his seat, coffee cup in hand. "There's something else as well."

"Oh?" Adam finished and pushed his plate aside.

"You know Dad – he's adamant that I should settle down and 'become a man'."

Adam laughed and nodded. "Oh yeah, I've heard him say that more than once. What does he mean, exactly? From what I can see, you're probably one of the most mature and responsible men I know."

Heath's lips pursed. "He thinks I should get married."

Adam rolled his eyes. "Marry who?"

"Anyone. Strike that – anyone *suitable*. He liked Chantelle."

Adam groaned and took another sip of coffee. "Chantelle? Really? You could do better."

"Maybe. But she's from a good family and she knows just how to charm my folks. She has them eating out of the palm of her hand, even though we've been broken up for months. Mom's constantly asking me if I've given any thought to calling 'that lovely Chantelle' up for another date."

Adam laughed. "I'm sorry, man. I guess they don't know her the way we do."

"The crux of it is, I don't think Dad's going to let me take the 'acting' off 'acting CEO' until I'm married." Heath chewed on his lower lip.

Adam absorbed his words. "You're kidding. Has he said that?"

"He's insinuated it." Heath frowned. "So there's a

family wedding coming up this weekend in Oregon – my cousin Newton – and Dad asked if I was bringing a date."

"Uh-huh?" Adam crossed his arms and arched an eyebrow. "And ..."

"And I told him I was. He'd just finished reaming me about my debauched single life and how I couldn't expect to lead the company while I'm still living like a bachelor ..."

Adam burst out laughing. "Debauched, you? Your dad really has no idea how boring you are, does he? Have you told him you're back in church yet."

Heath frowned and shook his head. "No clue. And no, I haven't. Mom knows, but I asked her not to tell anyone else yet." He shifted uncomfortably in his seat. "I guess I just want one thing Dad isn't part of, and I know what he'll say about it. I should tell him, I know, but I wanted to keep it to myself. At least for a while longer."

"So you have to find a date by this weekend. And it has to be someone who'd be willing to go away with you, even though you haven't been dating and they don't really know you?"

"Exactly."

Adam rubbed his neatly trimmed beard. "Well, that should be simple enough." He laughed. "Do you have anyone in mind?"

Heath's gaze roamed the diner and landed on Gwen's harried face. Perhaps? No, she'd never do it. He could be an axe murderer for all she knew.

Adam's eyes followed his gaze. "Who are you looking at? Oh, her? Yeah, she's cute."

Heath's cheeks flushed with warmth. "Beautiful, you mean."

Adam's eyebrows arched. "If you say so. Not really my type."

Heath grinned. "I was thinking of asking her."

"To Oregon for the weekend?" Adam took a sip of coffee. "Good luck with that. Do you even know her name?"

"Gwen."

"Well, I need to use the bathroom before we go back. You can ask her while I'm gone. Good luck." Adam winked, then stood and wandered toward the restrooms in the back of the diner.

As he passed the counter, a stack of red-and-white menus fell to the floor. Heath was up in a flash, dashing over to pick them up. Gwen got there at the same time, and they both bent to retrieve the laminated cards. "Thank you," she stated softly.

"You're welcome." He studied her face as he gathered the menus. He should ask now. But he couldn't just blurt it out – "hey, I know I'm a stranger, but would you go away with me and my entire family for the weekend?" He'd sound like a psychopath. No, it was a ridiculous idea. His father would just have to get over it. He didn't have a date, wouldn't have a date and they'd have to live with that. Perhaps he'd be single the rest of his life. What of it?

He sighed and set the menus on the counter, then ran his fingers through his hair. He glanced her way and found her studying him, her eyes bright and cheeks flushed. She busied herself with organizing the menus. "Is there anything else I can get you?"

He shook his head, but she wasn't looking. "Uh ... no, I just ... are you okay?"

She focused narrowed eyes on him, her eyebrows drawn together. "What?"

"You seem stressed. Is everything all right?"

There was a momentary glimmer in her eyes before she looked away. "I'm fine. Just a few financial issues."

"Oh?"

She managed a half-smile that disappeared quickly. "Waitressing doesn't pay as much as you might think," she quipped, her eyes flashing.

He laughed. "I'm sure that's true." She turned to walk away and his heart raced. It was now or never. "Actually, I have a proposal that might help you with your situation."

She faced him with one eyebrow arched.

He kept talking, worried he'd lose his nerve if he didn't. But his voice was low, not wanting the whole world to hear "I need a date."

She put her hands on her hips and cocked her head. "Mr. ..."

"Montgomery."

"Mr. Montgomery, I'm not sure what kind of woman you think I am ..."

His eyes flew wide. "No, no, I didn't mean ... that. I just need a date, nothing more. It's for my cousin's wedding, and my family is on my case. I'd pay you to come with me, all expenses, no pressure."

Her frown deepened. "Pay me? But why? I'm sure you could have your pick of women. Why not just ask one you know?"

He grimaced and ran a hand over his face. "That

would make more sense. But the thing is, the women I know ..." *Are either gold diggers, totally unsuitable or – in Chantelle's case – both.* "... it wouldn't go well. I thought it might be a better idea to pay someone I don't know. That way, there'd be no misunderstandings. It'd just be a transaction, an arrangement." Transactions, he understood. It would be business, not personal.

She opened her mouth, shut it, then opened it again, like a fish gasping for air. She was searching for a way to tell him no, he was sure. He shouldn't have said anything. She probably thought he was a complete creep, or worse ...

"So you'd pay me ... to spend the weekend pretending to be your fiancée?" Her voice was low but intense.

He nodded. He hadn't said *fiancée*, just *date*, but whatever. Either worked for him.

"At a wedding?"

"Yes, a family wedding. Everyone will be there – my Nana, my parents, brother, sister, aunts, uncles, cousins, friends ..." Might as well lay all his cards on the table now. It was a big favor he was asking – she should know what she was getting herself into if she agreed.

She nodded slowly, her brow furrowed. "Wow. Okay, here's the thing. I need to pay first month's rent to my new roommate. And I need a letter of recommendation ... something to tell her that I'm a good person, that I'll pay the rent on time, and I'm not going to set up a meth lab, that kind of thing."

He smiled. "I can do that."

"Where would we be going for the wedding?"

"Gleneden Beach, Oregon."

Her lips pursed. "Oregon ... it's nice there."

"So is that a yes?"

She chewed on her lower lip before replying. "That's a maybe. I'll have to think about it."

"If it makes you feel any better, I promise I don't have any expectations other than keeping my family off my back."

"In other words, I have to convince them we're together."

"And in love."

She arched an eyebrow. "All expenses paid, you said?"

He nodded. "Of course."

"When do you need an answer?"

Yesterday. "How about noon tomorrow?"

"Fine. I'll let you know tomorrow."

He reached out a hand and she shook it, then folded her arms. She looked so vulnerable standing there, he wanted to hug her and tell her everything would be okay. How had a woman like her gotten to a place in life where she didn't have rent money or anyone she could ask for a reference? He wished he could find out, but he could tell by the look on her face that she wasn't likely to share anytime soon. He'd have to earn her trust before she'd open up, that much was clear. Whether or not he could do that remained to be seen.

After Gwen scribbled down her phone number and address for him, Heath headed back to his table to find Adam waving the bill at him. He smiled and reached for his wallet. All he could do now was hope she'd agree to his plan. If she didn't, he wouldn't have much time to come up with a new one.

4

GWEN AWOKE TO THE SMELL OF TOAST AND DIANA'S humming. She smiled, then buried her face in the pillow for a second. It felt good to have a roof over her head, even if she was sleeping on a comforter on the floor. But for how long?

She got up and stretched with a yawn. One glance in the mirror revealed disheveled blonde hair piled on her head in a messy bun and dark smudges under her eyes. She'd lain awake until late thinking through the cowboy's proposal. Though why she still thought of him as a cowboy, she couldn't say. The last time she'd seen Heath Montgomery, he was dressed in an immaculate business suit. She almost hadn't recognized him.

She padded to the bathroom to freshen up, then joined Diana in the kitchen. Diana sat on a barstool at the counter, swinging one leg as she munched on a piece of toast, her iPad in front of her. "Good morning," she said with a smile, glancing in Gwen's direction.

"Morning. Thanks again for letting me move in so quickly."

Diana nodded. "I'm happy to have you here." She'd already reminded Gwen the previous evening that she'd given her until next week to come up with first month's rent. The reminder hung over Gwen's head like an axe. "There's cereal in the cabinet and bread by the toaster. I know you haven't had a chance to shop for groceries yet, so just help yourself."

Gwen smiled. "Thank you."

Diana nodded and returned her attention to her iPad and her toast.

Gwen decided on cereal and poured herself a bowl of Honey Bunches of Oats. As she added the milk, she considered Heath's invitation. Should she take him up on his offer? If she didn't, there was no way she could come up with the rent money by the end of the week. But to go to Oregon with a man she'd just met ...

Well, he seemed like a decent guy. Maybe she'd misjudged him the first time he came in, scruffy with three days of whiskers and dark circles under his eyes. He'd seemed like a man who'd never quite grown up. But freshly shaved and wearing a suit, he left a different impression altogether.

"What are you so deep in thought about?" asked Diana, taking a sip of orange juice.

Gwen carried her bowl of cereal to the counter and sat on the stool beside Diana. "I'm trying to decide whether to go on a date with a guy I just met."

Diana's eyebrows arched. "Oh? Is he cute?"

Gwen's cheeks burned. "Definitely. Maybe too cute."

"Is there such a thing?" asked Diana with a giggle.

Gwen laughed. "I suppose not. But he's sure of himself. I thought he was a cowboy at first, but yesterday he wore an expensive suit and he seems to work downtown, so I'm not sure."

"Sounds just about perfect to me."

"You think I should do it?"

"What's stopping you?"

"I just met him. I don't know anything about him. And I'd already decided I was going to stay away from men."

Diana chuckled. "Heartbroken?"

She nodded. "Divorced."

"Ugh. I'm divorced too – I know just what you mean."

Gwen took a bite of cereal and chewed it thoughtfully. "How long since yours?"

Diana carried her plate to the sink and rinsed it. "About two years."

"Does it get any easier?"

Diana's lips pursed and she tipped her head to one side. "Yeah, it does. It just takes time. And you shouldn't avoid men, just jerks. That's a rule everyone should live by."

Gwen's nosed wrinkled. "I'm with you on that one." Then her phone rang in her bedroom. She ran to unplug it from the wall where it was charging. "Hello?"

"Is this Gwen Alder?"

She didn't recognize the woman's voice, or the phone number. "Yes, this is she."

"I'm Lisa Connelly, vice-principal at Houghton

Elementary. We've e-mailed back and forth a few times in recent weeks ..."

Her new boss! A spark of adrenaline coursed through her veins. She needed this job so badly – it was the perfect opportunity to turn her life around. "Miss Connelly – how nice to finally speak with you."

"*Mrs.* Connelly, actually, but you can just call me Lisa. I hope this isn't a bad time ..."

"No, this is a fine time." She closed the bedroom door.

"I was hoping to show you around the school today, if you have time. I can give you the key to your classroom so you'll have time to set everything up before the students arrive. Also, we have a staff meeting Monday morning. All the staff will be here next week preparing for the new year, and we'll have several educational and self-improvement sessions for everyone to attend."

"That sounds wonderful. I'm free this morning if that works for you."

"Perfect." They arranged for Lisa to pick Gwen up outside her apartment in an hour and ended the call.

Gwen wandered back to the kitchen to finish breakfast with a broad smile on her face. Things were finally starting to look up.

∾

"So what do you think?" asked Lisa, leaning both hands on the chipped desk in front of her. Her long auburn hair hung neatly down her back and her pale green silk shirt and charcoal pencil skirt gave her a professional look Gwen was sure she could never pull off.

Gwen glanced around the classroom. It was clean and neat, if somewhat worn-looking. She smiled. "It's perfect. I'm so excited – I can't wait to start."

Lisa laughed. "I'm glad to hear it. We're looking forward to having you here. I think the third grade is just going to love Miss Alder."

Gwen wrapped her arms around herself and turned slowly to take it all in. There was a smartboard and rows of desks and chairs. Bookshelves lined one wall alongside open lockers where the students would hang their backpacks and coats. Back in Missoula, she'd taught first grade – this would be her first time as a third grade teacher. She'd missed having students over the summer and was more than ready to hang up her apron strings. Though the salary wasn't great – she'd likely be back at the diner again next summer.

Lisa glanced at her watch. "I'm sorry, I have to get going. My daughter's at a friend's house and my son is at soccer camp. I have to pick them both up and get home in time for the cable repair guy to show up." She chuckled. "Oh, the joys of domestic life."

Gwen smiled, but couldn't help feeling jealous. That was what she'd always wanted – children, domesticity. It was why she'd married so young, why she'd settled for Ed despite her doubts about him. She'd never have admitted it at the time, but looking back she could pinpoint the moments that'd sparked those doubts. After the wedding those questions were fanned into flames, but by then it was too late.

"No problem, I'm ready to head out. I'll come back and set up the classroom next week. Thanks for giving me the keys and showing me around – I really appreciate it. It's a lovely school." She jangled the keys in her pocket, imagining all the ways she would decorate the room if she had the money ... never mind, she'd make do with what she could find. Thankfully the previous teacher had left a lot of resources for the class.

She followed Lisa out to her car and climbed in. There was a small framed photograph dangling from the rear-view mirror of Lisa with her husband and children, smiling and making faces at the camera. "That photo's adorable."

Lisa chuckled. "I couldn't imagine life without them."

"You're a lucky woman." Gwen meant it. She was happy for Lisa – she just wished she could have something like what Lisa had. That wasn't wrong, was it?

An image of Heath's handsome face flashed before her. She still had to make a decision about whether to go away with him. She would see him today, and he'd be expecting an answer. Perhaps she should go. After all, what other options did she have – she needed the money. And he really did seem like a nice guy.

But then, Gwen mused, so had Edward.

GWEN STARED at her reflection in the bathroom mirror and took a slow breath as Katy Perry blasted from the living room stereo. Why was she so nervous? It wasn't like this was a date. She and Heath Montgomery were meeting to talk about their weekend away – a simple meeting to discuss a simple transaction. She was being hired as an actor, that was it. Shame she hadn't done any acting since Glee Club in high school.

She smoothed her bangs into place, then rested a hand on her uneasy stomach and looked at the clock. Heath was picking her up. Should she have driven herself? Him coming to her home made it seem even more like a date. She sighed and reached for her purse, slinging the strap over her shoulder, then headed to the living room and turned off the radio. Diana wasn't home – she worked as an accountant downtown. She locked the door behind her and headed for the parking lot.

When she reached it, she found Heath heading toward her. "Oh, Gwen – I was coming up to your apartment to get you."

She ran a hand over her hair nervously. "It's no problem. I decided to come out to meet you instead."

He shoved his hands into his pockets, seeming as nervous as she was. Like he wasn't sure what to say. "Well, let's go, then. Where would you like to eat?"

"I don't mind. Wherever you like."

"How about the Lucky Diner?" he asked, a twinkle in his blue eyes.

She laughed. "Anywhere but there."

In the end they agreed on a local sushi place, but when she went inside it didn't look like any restaurant she'd ever been to. Soft music floated throughout the immaculately-decorated space, and people leaned over tables speaking in hushed voices. Heath's hand brushed the small of her back as the maitre d' led them to a table. It sent a tingle up her spine. He wore a navy sports coat with fashionable jeans. She was in a summer dress, and as she glanced around she realized they were underdressed.

She took her seat and a waitress gracefully slid a napkin onto her lap. She ordered a mineral water, picked up a menu but noticed with a start that there were no prices listed. She swallowed, her heart racing. What if he expected her to pay? She only had forty dollars in her purse and her credit card was maxed out. "Uh ... this menu ..." She leaned toward Heath.

"Yes?" He looked at her over his own menu.

"There don't seem to be any ... prices listed."

He chuckled. "Yeah, they don't do that here for some reason. Don't worry about it, I'm paying."

She exhaled with relief. The server returned with her drink and she gulped down a mouthful to wet her dry throat.

They ordered and she did her best to act like she knew exactly what *ahi tuna nigiri* and *unagi* were. She'd only ever eaten a California roll before, and that from a corner stop-and-rob. Never mind – it was bound to be delicious.

She handed her menu to the waitress and took another sip of water, praying she'd be able to get through this lunch with the man across from her, let alone an entire weekend. She hadn't thought much about how gorgeous he was, but sitting across from him now, she was uniquely aware – and struggling to think of anything to say. Her mouth was refusing to cooperate.

Thankfully, he spoke first. "So are you new to the area?"

She nodded. "Yes, I've been here about a month."

"Oh? And you're just now finding a place to stay?"

She took a quick breath and her nose wrinkled. How to put this ... "I was living somewhere else, but then I had to find a new place ... quickly. So I've moved in with a lovely woman, Diana – she just needs first month and a letter of recommendation by next week."

"Yeah, you mentioned that. I'm happy to help. Have you been working as a waitress long?"

She laughed and made a face. "Yes and no. I've done it on and off for years, in high school and college. But now I'm a teacher, so I'm just waiting tables for the summer."

"Oh, you're a teacher?"

"Yes, I start at Houghton Elementary in just over a week."

"That sounds good. You must love kids."

She nodded, her body finally relaxing. "I do. They're great, you know? They don't pretend to be anyone other than who they are and they generally think that who they are is pretty good. They have fun without apology and they tell you what they think – no guessing games."

He chuckled and took a sip of water. "I can understand the virtue of that. It's one of the things I love about ranching, as well."

"Oh, you're a rancher? I wasn't sure. You wear a suit about as often as you do a cowboy hat, so ..."

He shrugged. "That's my life now. My father has a business downtown – he owns a number of ranches. I live on one of them, and work there whenever I can. But most of the time now I'm in the office. I like it too, but I wish sometimes I could be out on my horse more regularly, the way I used to."

She saw the nostalgia in his eyes and warmed to him. "So you love horses and ranching the way I love kids and teaching."

He nodded. "Sounds that way. Maybe we have more in common than you thought." He arched an eyebrow and met her gaze.

Her heart skittered. No, she couldn't feel that way about him, or any man. She was barely over her divorce. She would've been if Ed didn't keep inserting himself back into her life, making it harder to move on. It wasn't that she still cared for him, just that he reminded her of what she'd dreamed of and lost, of how much she'd been hurt. That's why she'd moved from Missoula to Billings – she needed some distance.

Trays of sushi were placed in front of each of them and Gwen eyed hers with suspicion. What was that stuff on top of it? How should she eat it? This didn't really seem like the kind of place where you'd eat with your hands. She glanced up to see what Heath did. He picked up a pair of chopsticks and used them to deftly dip a piece of sushi in soy sauce and pop it into his mouth.

She inhaled sharply and retrieved her chopsticks, fussing over how to hold them between her fingers.

"So have you thought about my proposal?" he asked, patting his mouth with a napkin.

Her face screwed up in concentration, she nodded. "Uh ... yes, of course." A piece of sushi fell from her chopsticks and landed with a splash in the soy sauce. Sheesh! They were slippery little suckers. And now it was drowning in sauce and she had brown spots on the front of her dress. Very graceful. She set down her chopsticks and gathered her thoughts. "I'm in."

His eyebrows shot skyward. "You are?"

"Sure. All I have to do is act for the weekend, right?"

He nodded. "That's it. Just convince everyone we're in love. I mean, it can't be that hard." He winked.

Her stomach flipped. "And you're paying."

"Yes."

"Plus first month's rent and writing me that letter."

"Yes and yes."

"And otherwise I'll be free to enjoy a weekend at some resort in Oregon?"

He laughed. "Yes, but you will have to spend quite a bit of time with my family. And they can be ... intense."

She laughed and picked up the chopsticks again, this time determined to get a mouthful. Her stomach growled and she stabbed a piece of sushi with one sticks. "I can handle family. Mine are no walk in the park." She bypassed the soy sauce, put the sushi into her mouth and ... ewww. The fish, or whatever it was, was completely raw. *Think happy thoughts. Think happy thoughts.* Hmmm ... not that bad once she got past the texture and the mystery.

He watched her with a little smile, eyebrows high. "You okay there?"

She nodded and swallowed. "Yeah."

"I've been meaning to ask – where is your family?"

Her throat tightened. She hated thinking about how much she missed them. "Dad passed a few years ago. Mom lives in Arizona."

"Is that where you grew up?"

She shook her head and aimed her chopsticks at another piece of sushi. "No, southern California, but I haven't lived there in years. Ed came from Montana ... "

"Ed?"

Her cheeks burned and she chewed her lower lip, still focused on getting the food to cooperate with her implements. "My ex-husband."

"You're divorced?"

She saw the look of surprise on his face and waited for the pity. That's how it always went. Next came the questions: how could you be divorced already? You're so young – what happened? Then the pity would give way to judgment. She chastised herself for bringing it up. "Yes. It's been a year since we separated. But only about six months since the divorce."

"I'm sorry."

She nodded. "Thanks." With a huff of frustration, she set down the chopsticks, picked up the sushi with her fingertips and stuffed it into her mouth.

They chatted comfortably through the rest of the meal and her inhibitions faded. He was easy to get along with, which was a surprise. But she was still trying to figure him out. Obviously he came from money, since his father owned more than one ranch, but she'd seen the truck he drove and the clothes he wore when he wasn't at work, and he looked working-class. Just how rich was he?

Well, it made no difference to Gwen. Just so long as he could pay her rent this once, that's all that mattered. He wasn't interested in more than that – he'd made that clear. And neither was she.

5

HEATH STEPPED OUT OF THE LIMOUSINE AND ADJUSTED his Stetson. He nodded to the driver and hustled up the path to Gwen's door, his heart pounding. And not just from the exercise. Ever since their lunch, he'd found his thoughts wandering to her. Her face would drift across his mind, or something she'd said would resurface in his memory and make him smile.

He shook his head. He was anxious about the weekend. It might be a complete disaster. He didn't know what he'd been thinking, paying someone to be his fiancée. But it was too late to back out now. He had an obligation to her and he would follow through with it, even if it was likely to blow up in his face. He walked up one flight of stairs, knocked on her door and stepped back, looking around. The building was old with red brick walls, but well-maintained and in a decent part of town.

When the door opened, he leaned against the frame with a grin. "Ready?"

Gwen nodded, blonde hair pulled back into a

ponytail and cheeks flushed pink with good health. "I'm ready." She patted the handle of her wheeled luggage and tugged a purse over her shoulder.

"Is this all?" he asked, reaching for the luggage.

"I've got it ..."

"No, I don't mind." He turned the luggage over and lifted it by its frayed leather handle. "I've got a car waiting downstairs to take us to the airport. I thought we could talk strategy on the plane."

"Strategy?"

"Well, if we're going to make it look like we're engaged, we should probably know more about each other."

"That's true, I suppose." She chewed the inside of her cheek.

"Don't worry, I promise I won't pry too much."

Gwen chuckled. "Just enough, huh? So where exactly are we going?" She glanced his way.

As her gaze met his, it sent a pulse of electricity through him. He masked his reaction with a cough. "Ahem ... it's called the Ariston Resort. It's in Gleneden Beach."

"Sounds fancy."

He laughed. "Yep. My cousin Newton is marrying his childhood sweetheart Heather Brownlow, and everything they do is fancy. But they're really nice – you'll love them. When you're not doing wedding stuff, feel free to enjoy the resort. I understand there are several pools, a spa, shopping close by and an amazing golf course. Plus the ocean, of course."

"What'll you do with your spare time?"

He shrugged. "Probably play golf. Dad and my

brother Dan both love it and they'll want to head out to the course every chance we get."

"So if things work out we might barely cross paths all weekend?" she quipped.

One eyebrow arched and he studied her face, unsure how serious she was. "I guess so." If he had it his way. She was cute and seemed nice enough, but all he needed was for her to do her part, convince his parents he was on a path to domestic bliss and land him the CEO role. He didn't want someone to bare his soul to or share a spiritual moment with, just act like a fiancée and otherwise leave him be.

He was ready to run Montgomery Ranches. His dad knew he was ready. This whole fake engagement was just something he'd have to push through, and one day look back and laugh about. Maybe Dad would laugh too.

Sure, he wanted to get married. One day, when he found the right woman, after he'd turned the company into the kind of business he dreamed it could be. But all that seemed to him like some kind of fairy tale. He'd almost given up on the idea since Chantelle. She'd opened his eyes to the truth – no matter what he did, how could he possibly find someone to love him for who he was?

He was a Montgomery – that was the heart of the matter. And everyone in Montana knew who the Montgomerys were and how much money they had. There was no getting past it. It seemed Gwen didn't know a thing about him – she'd acted as though she didn't – but she must be the only single woman in Montana who didn't recognize him on sight.

Especially after the Billings *Gazette* plastered his

smiling face on the front page and declared him the state's most eligible bachelor. He shook his head, remembering the fallout. He'd barely been able to get out of his truck and walk to the office without women darting out of the shadows to give him their number. It sounded like a dream come true to his friends, who teased him relentlessly about it, but to him it was a nightmare.

He stared out the window and watched the neighborhoods flash by. This was home. He loved living in Billings. But sometimes he wished he could get away and start over some place where no one knew the name Montgomery.

Billings Logan International Airport was small, and the private jet center even smaller. The driver pulled around the back of the hangar where parking spaces were marked out on the tarmac. He drew to a stop and Heath opened the door. "We're here."

Gwen got out and walked around to stand beside him, one hand shielding her eyes from the sun as she stared at the hangar in front of them. "Where are we?"

He frowned. "The airport."

"This isn't the airport. I've been to the airport before. There's a food court and lines and airplanes on the tarmac ..."

"That's over there. This is Edwards Jet Center. We keep the company jet here."

Her eyebrows arched. "You have a jet?"

He nodded. "The company does. I use it when I need to, and so do board members or executives." The driver walked toward the hanger with Gwen's luggage and Heath set off after him, scanning his phone for missed calls. Two from Dan, who was Montgomery

Ranches' chief legal counsel as well as Heath's younger brother. No doubt he was calling to ask when Heath was heading out, since he'd left for the resort earlier in the week. Two more from Adam – what were those about?

"Is this our plane?" Gwen jogged up beside him, her flats slapping against the tarmac.

Heath glanced at the jet, then nodded in assent. "Yes. I'm sorry, I have to make a call. Excuse me." He ducked off to one side and put the phone to his ear as it rang. The weekend away couldn't have come at a worse time – things at work were so busy, he couldn't afford a second straight weekend offsite. But family was important to his folks – they'd repeated that over and over throughout his childhood and his early adult years. *Family mattered.* Whatever was going on at work, they always made the effort to attend important family events.

And they expected him to be there as well. So he just had to get through this weekend and catch up with work on Monday. Then, if everything went the way it should, Dad would announce him as CEO at the next board meeting and his future would begin to fall into place.

"Adam? It's Heath. What's up?"

Gwen watched Heath pace across the tarmac beside the jet, the phone to his ear and his voice a dull murmur that echoed around the cavernous hangar. What should she do? Climb on board the jet? Stand where she was and wait? She had no idea what the etiquette was in this situation. What was she thinking? She had to pretend to be the fiancée of a billionaire cowboy for an entire weekend? There's no way she could pull that off – she couldn't even decide whether to board the jet or stand around like a fool in the hangar.

The driver walked by again, this time carrying Heath's luggage – a small backpack, a suit bag and a laptop case. She frowned – in comparison, it looked like she'd packed for a month-long getaway – but she'd had no idea what to bring.

Worse still, she'd come to the grim realization that she didn't own anything nice. Her entire closet was a wasteland. She groaned inwardly, thinking of the dress she'd picked to wear to the wedding, a navy blue slip dress. It was too old, and by the time they arrived it'd be wrinkled as well. She'd worn it dozens of times to weddings, parties and more over the years, and had always loved it. But now, looking up at the gleaming white sides of the jet, she knew it wouldn't be suitable.

A flight attendant walked by and smiled at her, then climbed the staircase at the front of the jet and disappeared through the door. Maybe she should follow ...

Just then, Heath hung up the phone and hurried to her side. "Sorry about that," he said, cupping her elbow with his hand and guiding her toward the stairs. "You could've boarded."

She smiled. "I wasn't sure."

The inside of the jet was even more impressive than the outside. "Sit anywhere you like," said Heath behind her.

She nodded and chose a seat against the left wall

of the cabin – more like a couch, really. She ran her hand over the soft leather as Heath sat across from her, his eyes still on his phone screen. "Will your parents be joining us?"

He glanced at her. "No. They left earlier in the week. Dad and my brother Dan wanted to get a couple of golf games in before the rest of us arrived." He chuckled. "Dad likes to think the practice will help him win."

The plane's engine rumbled to life and the pilot announced their departure over the PA, soon replaced by the soft strains of background music. The flight attendant took their drink orders, and before she knew it the plane was in the air. She studied Heath, who sipped his drink and acted as though he hadn't noticed the plane move beneath them. "You said something about us getting to know each other better?"

He met her gaze, then put his phone in his jeans pocket. "I think it'd be a good idea. Otherwise there's no way we can pull this off. Mom and Nana will be all over you with questions."

She swallowed. "Okay, so what would you like to know?"

He leaned forward and set his elbows on his thighs. "What's your middle name?"

She smiled. "Rose."

"Okay, Gwen Rose Alder."

"Yep. And you?"

"Roderick."

"No way!"

He covered his face with his hands and mumbled against them. "My great-grandfather's name – I couldn't make it up if I tried." He laughed and rubbed his palms on his jeans.

She chuckled. "I like it. It's very regal."

"I never thought of it like that."

"What else?" she asked, crossing one leg over the other.

He ran a hand through his hair. "Let's see ... where were you born?"

"Long Beach, California."

"Oh? Is there really so much drama in the LBC?" His eyes sparkled.

She couldn't help smiling at the Snoop Dogg quote. "Not while I was there – it was pretty quiet. But Snoop and I lived in different parts of town."

"That would explain it. I was born in Billings – been there all my life. No famous rappers in my neighborhood either." She burst out laughing and he joined her. "We should probably talk about how we met," he continued, leaning back in his seat.

She nodded. "We could say we met at the diner, so we wouldn't have to make it up entirely. They say when you lie, you should tell as much truth as possible so you don't get caught out."

He frowned. "Remind me not to trust a thing you say."

She laughed. "Oh, I hardly ever lie. Honest."

"And now I'll never really know." He winked. Was he flirting with her? She couldn't really say, but whatever it was, she liked it. He was fun, not the stuck-up, rich guy she'd thought he might be.

They spent the next hour sharing trivia about themselves. She purposefully steered him away from questions about her marriage – she didn't want to talk about it. Surely it wouldn't come up in conversation, not at a family wedding.

When the plane landed at the tiny airport in Gleneden Beach, Gwen was almost sorry. It wouldn't just be them sharing light-hearted banter any longer – now she'd have to face the rest of the family and play the role of a happy-in-love fiancée. She forced a smile and stepped out of the plane.

THE CAB PULLED up to the resort and Gwen's mouth fell open. Green acreage stretched as far as she could see in every direction. Slowly sloping golf causeways rose and fell, richly leaved trees softening the landscape. The resort's main building nestled among the hills as though it had grown there. Sandstone mixed with softly painted bricks and gold accents gave the resort a luxurious but warmly welcoming feel. A sign etched into sandstone at the entrance read *Ariston Golf Resort*.

Heath opened the door of the car and offered her his hand. She took it, stepping out into the warm Oregon day. They were a happy couple, in love, ready to face the world.

Gwen swallowed as a woman in a lavender and gray silk dress with a straw hat perched on her head bustled toward them. Her blue eyes twinkled as she smiled. "You're here!" she trilled, kissing Heath on the cheek. She took Gwen's hands and studied her. "You must be Gwen. Heath's told us all about you – well, not all but some, and we're dying to know the rest. I can't believe you're engaged and we've never even met you! You must think us so rude, but honestly, getting information out of this boy is like pulling teeth. We're so thrilled you're going to be part of our family!"

"Now, now, Arlene – give the girl a chance to take a breath before you grill her." Gwen glanced up to see a tall man with silver hair and dark brown eyes. He looked a lot like Heath. "I'm Graham Montgomery, Heath's dad. It's a pleasure to meet you, Gwen." He held out a hand and Gwen shook it firmly as he eyed Heath. "And such a surprise to hear you're betrothed to my eldest son." Arlene jabbed him in the side with her elbow, and he coughed. "Pleasantly surprised, of course."

"And it's wonderful to meet you, Mr. Montgomery," Gwen replied.

"Oh, please call us Graham and Arlene," Arlene insisted.

Gwen ducked her head. "All right, thank you. I will."

Arlene took Gwen's arm and led her into the resort through the open front doors. Tall potted plants loomed on either side and a long reception desk peeled away to the left. "Don't worry about checking in, darling," she called over her shoulder to Heath. "We've already done that for you." Then she bent her head toward Gwen's with a conspiratorial whisper. "We have adjoining rooms. We can tap messages in Morse code to each other through the walls. Won't that be fun?"

Gwen had to bite her lip to keep from giggling.

Arlene pulled up short and grabbed Gwen's hand, holding it up to the light. "Oh dear, your ring is gone!"

Gwen's eyebrows arched. She glanced at Heath,

who was just catching up, but found no help there. "Well, his proposal was so impulsive, he hasn't had time to buy one."

Heath shoved his hands into his pockets. "That's right, Mom. As soon as we get a chance, we'll go shopping."

Arlene frowned. "That's not very romantic, Heath. You should have the ring with you when you propose to a woman."

"Leave the boy be, Arlene," Graham scolded. "At least he actually popped the question. Though it might have been nice for him to tell us he was dating and let us meet the girl."

Heath sighed and slapped a hand to his forehead. "Okay, Mom, Dad, I get it. You're right – I should've told you. And I should've bought the ring before I proposed. But you've wanted me to find someone for so long, surely you can't complain about how I do it."

Arlene's nostrils flared and she patted Gwen's hand, which she still held. "Yes, darling, that's true – I'm happy to have a new daughter, regardless of how it happened."

"Wonderful. Now can we please find our room? I know Dad is dying to get out on the course – I can almost see his forehead twitching."

"I'm not desperate," Graham grumbled, his hands on his hips. "But the weather is perfect and we don't want to waste the daylight."

Heath chuckled. "Let's go, then."

6

GWEN FLICKED THROUGH THE CHANNELS AND SIGHED. The bed was so soft and luxurious she could lay there forever. Finally she settled on a classic movie, *An Affair to Remember*, and laid her head back on the mountain of pillows. Why couldn't men be like Cary Grant – tall, dark, passionate and romantic? She sighed, lifted a champagne glass and sipped, then plucked a strawberry from the bowl beside her and ate it slowly, her eyes fixed on the screen. This was the life.

Arlene and Graham had the champagne and strawberries sent up to her room so they could all celebrate the engagement. After they'd each had a glass and a few bites, Arlene had retreated to her room for a rest and the men had changed and gone out for a game of golf. She'd been relieved to discover Heath's parents were old-fashioned enough to rent separate rooms for her and Heath. Otherwise one of them would've been sleeping on the floor. As delicious as the mattress felt beneath her, that would've been a tragedy.

She sighed again and reached for another strawberry, rubbing one foot on the soft hem of her bathrobe.

There was a rap at the door and she bolted upright, set the glass down on the table and padded to the door, still chewing. Heath leaned against the door frame with a glint in his eyes. "I see you're enjoying yourself."

She laughed. "I sure am. And you?"

He shrugged. "It was a good game. I won. Dad wasn't happy." He grinned.

"Strawberry?" she asked, stepping aside and waving toward the half-empty bowl.

He laughed. "No thanks. I just came by to let you know we're all having dinner together. I thought you might like some time to get dressed."

Her eyes widened. "Is it formal? Or can I wear jeans?"

"Hmmm ... did you bring any evening gowns?"

She scratched her chin. "Well ... come in, I'll show you what I've got."

He followed her and shut the door. She opened the closet, where she'd hung the gown she'd brought for the wedding, alongside some light summer dresses, shirts, skirts and jeans.

He frowned. "How about I take you shopping?"

"Shopping? Where?"

"There's a boutique downstairs. We could look there."

"I don't know ..." Should she? It was just dinner. How formal could it really be?

"I'm buying."

Her eyes widened. "Let's go."

He laughed and turned to go. "I'll be waiting outside. Just throw something on and join me."

Ten minutes later she felt like Julia Roberts in *Pretty Woman*, only without the streetwalking. On the ground floor of the resort were three separate boutiques – one carrying expensive resort wear, another evening gowns and the third various brand name clothes ranging from casual to semi-formal. Heath had led her directly to the evening wear.

He sat in a chair, once again engrossed in his phone, while the saleswoman gathered an impressive array of gowns for her to try on. "Do you like green?" she asked, holding an emerald gown with one shoulder strap against Gwen's frame.

"It's ... beautiful." She glanced at Heath, hoping he'd weigh in, but he wasn't looking. "How many should I buy?" she asked him.

"Three should do it," he mumbled, his attention on whatever he was tapping on the screen.

She frowned. Fine. If he wasn't going to help, she'd just pick what she liked. She tried on more than two dozen dresses, finally narrowing it down to three – a burnt orange strapless dress in silk, with a fitted bodice and long flowing skirt, a sea-blue sheath with spaghetti straps that clung to her, and (in honor of Julia) a deep red gown with a plunging neckline and a short train. They were easily the three most beautiful items of clothing she'd ever worn.

She glanced at the price tags and almost gagged on the glass of water the saleswoman had brought her. But hey, Heath was paying. She wore the burnt orange dress out of the store, along with a pair of nude pumps the saleswoman helped her pick out. It should do nicely for the family dinner.

When she stepped outside the store, Heath was on the phone. He saw her and his jaw dropped. "Sorry, Adam, got to go." He hung up the phone and put it in his pocket. "Wow."

She grinned shyly. "Do you like it?" She swished from side to side, feeling the silk play around her legs.

"It's stunning." He walked toward her, eyes still wide. "You look amazing."

When he offered her his arm, she could've been a princess. She held onto it as he walked her back up to her room. "Thank you for the dresses."

He shook his head. "My pleasure. That one was made for you. I'm going to go get dressed myself and I'll pick you up in half an hour. Does that sound okay?"

She nodded. "Perfect."

As he walked away, Gwen watched him go, appreciating just how well his jeans fit to his muscular thighs and the way his dark hair curled a little over his collar. She smiled as she waltzed back into her room. Time to do her hair and makeup. She couldn't wait to see the look on his face in thirty minutes.

WHEN HE CAME by her room to collect her, he was dressed in a suit with no tie. His white shirt had the top button undone and his brown hair looked freshly washed, falling softly over his forehead. "I'm afraid you'll outshine the bride," he whispered in her ear as she put her hand into the crook of his arm.

She grinned and shivers ran up and down her body.

Downstairs, he introduced her one by one to his family, all seated around a long trestle table in the center of the restaurant. The bride and groom were glowing happily and welcomed her warmly. When she'd made the rounds, she finally sat between Heath's Nana and his sister Samantha, with Heath directly across from her. He studied her with concern, his gaze flitting between the three women. What was he worried about? Everything would be fine.

"So you're the young lady who's captured my Heath's heart," said Nana, her bright blue eyes fixed on Gwen.

Gwen nodded and swallowed the piece of bread she'd been chewing. "Yes, ma'am." She shook Nana's hand with a smile.

"I hope the two of you will be just as happy as my Herb and I were. He died fifteen years ago, you know. Don't let that happen – don't let him die first. It's terrible to be all alone in your twilight years."

Gwen chewed her lower lip and nodded solemnly. "Yes, ma'am, I imagine it is."

"What do you do for a living, dear?"

"I'm a teacher."

"A teacher, did you say?" chimed in Samantha.

"Yes, third grade."

"Oh, that sounds like fun. I'm a doctor – nothing fun about that." She made a face.

"I'm sure it must be fun sometimes ..."

"Not with what I do. I'm a GP. I should've been a

surgeon – at least then I'd get to cut people open. But no, instead I decided to be a GP, so I get to wipe snotty noses all day long." She grimaced and reached for a roll.

"It can't be all bad." Gwen wanted to make a good impression, but she could tell Samantha wasn't going to make it easy.

"I'm being facetious." Samantha sighed. "I do that sometimes. Brett, my boyfriend, says I use it as a coping mechanism. But he's a psychiatrist, so he would say something like that, wouldn't he?"

Gwen arched an eyebrow and nodded. "I guess so." She was so out of her depth she was treading water. She looked for Heath. He seemed to have disappeared.

"And do you plan to stay home once you have children, dear?" asked Nana, taking a sip of iced tea.

Gwen's eyes widened. "Um ... I don't know yet. I hadn't thought much about it ..."

"She'll want to work," Sam insisted. "But it wouldn't make sense. Heath's job keeps him out all hours and you know the way things are, Nana. It's the women who end up having to hold down the home front, no matter what the feminists try to tell us."

Gwen took a sip of her iced tea, her heart pounding. Where was Heath when she needed him? He was on the other side of the room, deep in conversation with one of his uncles – Steve, Andrew, Phil? She couldn't remember. And she was beginning to sweat – what if she stained her new dress with her armpit sweat? She lifted her arms slightly and tried to blow air beneath them.

"Now, dear Samantha, don't get going with all that

feminist nonsense. When I was a young woman, we knew what our roles were. We stayed home and raised the children and our husbands went to work to make the dough. It worked for us, and I don't see why it wouldn't work the same way for you younguns."

Sam sighed and rolled her eyes. "Oh, Nana, you don't understand. I make just as much money as Brett does."

"I'm sure when the time comes, we'll make the decision together," Gwen said, hoping to change the subject. "Do you ride, Sam?"

"Ride?"

"Horses. Heath said you grew up on a ranch."

Sam smiled, the tension seeming to slip away as she leaned forward. "Yes, I love to ride. Do you?"

Gwen took a quick breath. "Uh, no. I've never gotten the chance to learn."

Nana piped up again. "Tell me, dear. How did you and Heath meet? I want to hear all about it."

Just then she felt Heath's hands on her shoulders. She looked up to see him standing behind her chair. He winked and she felt a rush of warmth. "Actually, it's kind of a funny story ..."

"Oh?" Sam leaned in.

"Did I hear something about a story?" asked Arlene, rushing over and taking Heath's seat at the table. She set her wine glass down, her eyes eager.

"I was going to tell Nana about how Heath and I met," said Gwen, her thoughts swirling. She had to come up with something at least vaguely interesting, something that would make it seem as though they'd genuinely fallen head over heels in love so quickly they'd forgotten the engagement ring. "I mentioned

I'm a teacher, but I haven't started my new job yet. So for the summer, I've been waitressing at a diner downtown."

Nana nodded, still smiling. "That sounds nice, dear."

"One day Heath came in with some of his friends and ordered breakfast. He ordered waffles, and when I brought him his order I slipped on some spilled juice and dumped the whole thing in his lap."

Arlene's eyebrows arched high. "Oh! Now that's an interesting way to make an impression."

Heath squeezed her shoulders, and she glanced up to see his eyes narrow. She frowned, then continued.

"He jumped up, squealing ..."

"I don't know that it was quite a squeal ..." he interrupted with an uncomfortable chuckle.

But she was on a roll. "Pumpkin, your voice was so high I thought the windows might shatter."

The women around her erupted in fits of laughter. "Oh dear," sputtered Nana when she could catch her breath again. "Then what happened?"

Gwen caught Heath's eye and read his exasperation. She resisted a smile and reached for his hand as she stood to face the group. "I apologized, of course – I was mortified. I grabbed a dish cloth from the kitchen and hurried to help. But when I tried to wipe the syrup from his pants, he leaped away with a yelp. I knew right away I'd done something inappropriate. But as he jumped, he slipped on the wet end of a mop one of the other waitresses had left propped up against the counter. The mop stick popped him right in the nose ..."

Heath squeezed her hand a little tighter, and he cocked his head to one side, frowning as if to try and shut her up.

She patted his hand. "Don't worry, pumpkin, I'm not going to tell them about that poor woman."

By now the ladies were gasping for breath as their laughter echoed throughout the restaurant. "What ... woman ...?" cried Arlene, a hand to her side.

Gwen pursed her lips as though she didn't wish to say, then shook her head. "This woman was having breakfast with her colleagues in another booth. She was wearing the prettiest red suit with matching pumps, wasn't she, pumpkin?"

Heath's nostrils flared. "I couldn't say ..." She could tell he wasn't pleased with her story, but if he was going to engage her in a complicated lie to his family, he could at least let her have some fun with it. And they were eating it up.

"Well, when the mop hit him, he stumbled backward and tripped on the woman's pumps He fell, flapping his arms like a bird taking off, and knocked her pancakes, scrambled eggs and coffee all over her. She was covered from head to toe in her breakfast, and she was *not* happy, let me tell you. My manager came out, breathing fire, and I had to comp her meal."

By this time most of the table had stopped what they were doing to listen to and laugh at the story. Heath took a quick breath, now squeezing her hand so hard she thought it might lose feeling.

She pulled herself from his grasp and patted his arm lovingly. "Now, Heath didn't have to say a word – he could've let me take the heat. But instead, he smoothed things over with my manager and promised to cover the woman's dry cleaning bill. And that's when I thought he might be the man for me. Good-looking, generous and humble – well, it's hard to find a man like that. I didn't know his name or anything else about him, but I knew he was something else. Then after he helped me clean up the mess, he asked me out. And the rest is history."

That seemed to mollify Heath – his smile looked genuine. And the rest of the group's mirth subsided. Graham extracted a handkerchief from his pants pocket and wiped his eyes dry. He hadn't laughed as much as the rest of the group, but enough that his eyes were filled with tears. "I can't say I've ever heard a story quite like that – or anything remotely similar about my son before. Perhaps there's more to Heath than any of us knows. But I'm glad he met you, Gwen. And I'm certain the two of you will be happy together."

Just then, Gwen noticed the perturbed look on the bride's face and cleared her throat. "But enough about us – tonight we're here to celebrate Newton and Heather's impending nuptials. So let's drink a toast to the happy couple!"

Everyone obediently reached for a glass and raised it high, echoing her words. "To the happy couple!"

Heather smiled and her cheeks flushed pink. She nodded thanks and spun around to kiss her intended on the lips.

❧

HEATH STUDIED Gwen as she sipped champagne and

chatted quietly with several members of his family. He frowned – she got along with his kin better than he did. Apart from the story of how they met, which he fully intended to talk to her about, she'd been polite, friendly, everything he could've asked. She was living up to her promise to be his fake fiancée. So why wasn't he feeling better about it?

Likely it was because he hated lying to his family. Especially Nana, who'd been so excited when he told her he was engaged. He hadn't thought it through enough before he made his plans, hadn't fully considered how his lie might hurt hers or his parents' feelings. He wished he'd never come up with the cockeyed plan, and now that it was in place he couldn't back out. He wasn't sure his family would forgive him if they discovered what he'd done, at least not for a long time.

He shook his head and chugged the last of the sweet tea in his glass. He had to stop worrying about it – there was a method to his madness. He wanted to be CEO of Montgomery Ranches. He'd earned it, working hard for years ... well, working there for years, hard over the past two. His father handing over the reins was what everyone at the company expected, and what he'd promised, so many times he'd lost count. Yet now that the time had come, Dad was holding back.

He'd wondered often over recent months if his father lacked faith in his ability, or if his offhand comments about settling down and getting married were the one thing standing in the way. Well, at least now he'd find out. If Dad retired and handed Heath the position, he'd know it was because of his relationship with Gwen, not a lack of faith in his eldest son's abilities.

He sighed and ran a hand through his hair as Gwen trotted unsteadily to his side. "A little too much champagne?" he asked, with one eyebrow raised.

She shook her head. "No, it's these heels. I never wear anything this high."

He chuckled. "Well, at least we don't have far to go – just to the elevators and down the hall to your room. You should be able to make it, right?"

She nodded and set her glass on the table. "I'm ready if you are."

He offered her his arm and she slid her hand through the crook, resting it against his sleeve. It felt natural, good, and his heart melted in his chest. "Let's go."

They waved goodnight to the rest of the family and headed for the small bank of elevators near the reception desk. Every few steps, he felt her lean more heavily on his arm. She really couldn't manage those shoes. "Thank you for tonight," he began.

She interrupted with a chortle. "Did I do okay, boss?"

He rolled his eyes. "You did fine. Though I could've done without the theatrical stories."

She stifled a laugh. "Yes, sir."

His eyes narrowed. "Don't call me 'sir'."

"Sorry, sir ... I mean, boss." She chuckled.

He sighed. "You're impossible."

The elevator opened and they stepped inside, her hand still on his arm. "Then what would you like me to call you? I mean, you are my employer, aren't you?"

The doors closed behind them and he let his eyes drift shut as well. "You're giving me a headache."

"Sorry, boss, I'll work on that." She giggled and covered her mouth to muffle the sound.

He studied her a moment. Clearly the heels weren't the only reason for her unsteadiness. "Do you think you could take things down a notch? I mean, you're doing a great job, you've got everyone convinced we're engaged – which is exactly what I asked, so I can't really complain. But I don't want them all to fall in love with you."

Her brow furrowed. "You don't want them to like me? But would they believe you'd be engaged to someone they didn't like?"

He bit his lip. "I don't know. This is all new territory to me. But I can't help thinking that if you make them love you too much, they'll be devastated when we break up. So perhaps you could be a little less charming, maybe even a bit sullen. That way, when we do break up, they'll understand – perhaps they won't even blame me."

She sighed and tugged her hand away from his arm, letting it hang limp at her side. "Whatever you say, boss."

"And don't call me 'boss'."

"Yes, sir."

His eyes rolled. She really was impossible.

The elevator doors dinged open and he walked her to her room. She retrieved her key from her purse and stuck it in the door lock. "Anything else I should know before tomorrow?"

He shook his head and stuffed his hands deep into his pants pockets. "No."

She faced him, her expression sincere. "And thank you again for the dresses. They're really beautiful."

He nodded. "You're welcome. You make them beautiful."

Her eyes widened as the door shut behind her.

Heath exhaled slowly, then wandered down the hall to his room. Only a few feet of carpet separated their rooms, but it felt like a galaxy stood between them. The more he got to know her, the more he felt as though he knew nothing about her. And even with the way she irked him, the more he wanted to know.

7

GWEN OPENED HER EYES AND GLANCED AROUND THE room. It took a few moments to remember where she was, but when she did she smiled. She breathed deeply and stretched both arms and legs as far across the king-sized mattress as she could, grinning with glee. The bed was so comfortable. And her room was enormous, holding the canopy bed, a small sitting area and a television. There was a Jacuzzi in the spacious bathroom, as well as a shower and double vanity. And the patio looked out over the sloping green hills of the golf course.

She stood with a yawn and padded over to the windows, pulling the curtains back and letting the sunshine in. Birds called outside the glass and she flicked on the TV, turning to a morning talk show she never got to watch because she was either teaching, or sleeping after a late shift at the diner.

After a hot shower, she dressed in a turquoise bikini she'd gotten on sale the previous summer and threw a flowing white knee-length dress over it. She grabbed her sunhat, Kindle, purse and beach towel, put on flip-flops and headed for the door. She'd spotted three swimming pools on one side of the resort the day before and she intended to make good use of them just as soon as she'd eaten breakfast.

In the hallway, she spied Arlene and Graham in front of Heath's door. Graham had one hand poised, ready to knock. "Good morning."

Both turned to look at her, and Arlene smiled. "Gwen, good morning to you as well. Isn't it a beautiful day?"

"Are you looking for Heath?" she asked, slipping her room key into her purse.

Arlene nodded and Graham frowned. "Yes, we are. Have you seen him this morning ...?"

Just then the door opened and Heath stood there. He arched an eyebrow at the three of them on the threshold. "Hello."

"Good morning, dear," Arlene replied. "We came to see if you'd like to join us for breakfast."

He frowned, and Gwen noticed the cell phone in his hand. "Just a moment," he said, stepping away from the door. She heard the murmur of his voice as he finished up a phone call before reappearing. "Sorry about that. Work. Sure, I'd love to have some breakfast – I'm starving."

"Who was that?" asked Graham.

"Adam – he's checking into something for me."

"Anything I should worry about?"

Heath shook his head. "Nope. Let's go." He pulled the door shut behind him, then nodded at Gwen.

She glanced at his parents, who were both watching them with great interest. "Good morning, pumpkin." She stepped forward and planted a kiss on his lips. His eyes flew wide in surprise, and her heart skipped a beat as their lips met.

When she pulled away, Graham slapped him on the back with a chuckle. "Come on, son, you've got to put more into it than that if you intend to keep the spark in your marriage."

Arlene nodded in agreement. "Marriage takes work, hon. And a wife needs to feel as though she's adored." She arched an eyebrow and caught her husband's eye. He shook his head and pursed his lips.

Heath frowned at Gwen, but she shrugged, turned and strutted down the hall. What was he upset about? He was paying her to make sure everyone believed they were engaged – he could hardly think the cool greeting he'd given her would be good enough.

The four of them entered the elevator together and she put her hand in his. He glanced down at it, then met her gaze. "What's wrong, pumpkin?" she asked with a smile. "You seem tense. You really should relax. After all, this is supposed to be a vacation."

A muscle in his jaw twitched and he bobbed his head in assent.

"That's right, hon. You really shouldn't work so hard," Arlene agreed. "Everyone needs time off."

"Yes, Mom," he said as he laced his fingers through Gwen's, sending a bolt of electricity through her.

AFTER BREAKFAST, Gwen retreated to the side of the main pool. She laid her towel down on a pool chair

and settled into it, booting up her Kindle to read the
latest Claire Kelley mystery. She paused to glance up
at the balconies overhead. Heath's was up there, and
she could picture him, cell phone attached to his ear.
She shook her head. He worked more than anyone
she'd ever known – a weekend at a resort in Oregon
and he was up in his room, likely hunched over his
laptop.

Never mind. She had no intention of wasting this
opportunity – she'd take advantage of every luxury
the resort had to offer. She couldn't remember the last
time she'd had a vacation, not counting camping out
of the back of Ed's truck in eastern Montana. She
spent a good part of the morning swimming, sipping
drinks brought to her by the pool wait staff, lounging
and reading her book.

Just before lunch, Arlene and Samantha showed
up, each in cool resort dresses that flapped around
their slim legs as they walked. Samantha glanced
down at Gwen over the top of her Ray-Bans. "We're
headed to the spa and Mom thought you might like to
join us, sis."

Gwen lifted the brim of her hat. "The spa?"

"We've booked massages, but I'm sure they could
fit you in as well," Arlene told her.

"And a facial and seaweed-and-mud wrap," added
Samantha with a flip of her hand.

A massage and a facial? Gwen jumped to her feet
and dumped her Kindle into her purse. "That sounds
just about perfect. I'd love to join you."

They walked to the end of the pool where a sign
above a glass door read *Ariston Spa*. Inside, they sat on
a row of chairs to await their appointments. Gwen had

no trouble adding her name to the appointment book. She flipped through a magazine, then felt Samantha's eyes on her and met her stare.

"So what is it about you?" Samantha wondered.

"Sam!" chastised Arlene, resting a hand on Samantha's leg.

"What do you mean?" asked Gwen, her brow furrowed.

"Heath's only ever brought one woman home before to meet the family – Chantelle. But after only knowing you a few short weeks, he's asked you to marry him and invited you to a family wedding. Why?"

Arlene tutted and shook her head at her daughter. "Sam, it's not your place ..."

"Mom, I want to know."

Gwen swallowed hard and set the magazine down on the table beside her. "I don't know. To be honest with you, it has been a whirlwind. But Heath's a great guy – I mean, you know that. But he's the kind of guy that a woman can fall in love with that fast. As to what he sees in me, I couldn't say. Perhaps you should ask him."

What else could she say? It wasn't a strange question to ask, given the circumstances. She couldn't fault their suspicions – they'd never heard of her before, and all of a sudden she was engaged to Heath. She was also surprised to hear he'd only introduced them to one former girlfriend. Yes, he seemed closed off, but so much that he wouldn't let *anyone* get close? What had happened to make him that way?

"Leave Gwen be," responded Arlene, red spots warming her cheeks. "If Heath loves her, that's good enough for me. And it should be good enough for you."

Sam nodded silently, but Gwen could see the doubt in her eyes. And she couldn't blame her.

HEATH STUDIED the spreadsheet on his laptop screen and rubbed his eyes. The numbers were beginning to blur together, and he still couldn't figure what was going on. Something just didn't add up. And he still had the monthly financial reports to review and staff travel requests to approve.

Being at the top meant a never-ending stream of requests came his way all hours of the day and night. He could work twenty-four hours a day and never get it all done. He'd fought against hiring a full-time assistant, instead sharing Judy with Adam, but perhaps it was time he took the plunge. He hated the thought of having to train someone new – it seemed like just another task to add to his infinite to-do list. But if he didn't do something soon, that list would suffocate him. And he'd have to train someone when Judy went on maternity leave anyway.

A knock at the door broke through his reverie and he stood with a groan, stretching his hands over his head. Hunching over a coffee table wasn't the best way to work. "Coming," he called before slouching toward the door.

Gwen stood in the doorway with a smile, her face glowing. "Howdy, boss!"

"Hi. What time is it?" His stomach contracted with

hunger, and he was suddenly aware that he hadn't eaten since breakfast.

"It's lunchtime. Are you coming down to the restaurant? Everyone else is already there, but I thought maybe we could set tongues wagging and get a table to ourselves." She waggled her eyebrows.

He chuckled and ran a hand over his face. "That sounds great. Let me just grab my wallet."

When he returned to the door, she studied him under hooded eyes. "You work too hard."

He frowned. "There's a lot to get done."

"I'm sure that's true, but everyone needs a break now and then."

He grunted and held the elevator door open for her.

She stepped inside and turned to face him. "I've got an idea. We're only here for a couple of days, so how about after lunch you set work aside and take me out for a round of golf?"

He really should go back to his room to take that conference call Adam had organized with the finance team. But perhaps she was right. It *was* beautiful at the resort. He could get Adam to postpone the call. After all, what good was it to be acting CEO if you couldn't move things around to suit your own schedule? "Okay." The elevator dinged and the doors slid open. "Do you play golf?"

She shook her head. "Never have."

He raised an eyebrow. "I guess I can show you ..."

"That would be great."

They walked together to the restaurant. Gwen linked her fingers through his and he found he liked it more than he'd thought he would. She was so different, so unlike anyone he'd ever dated before. Not that they were actually dating ... but still, he couldn't help thinking about it. What if they were together?

No, it would just complicate things. She didn't see him that way – she made that clear every time she called him *boss*. He was paying her to be his fiancée for a weekend, that was the extent of their relationship. Still, his hand tingled where it touched hers and his thoughts strayed to how her silken hair would feel against his skin and how tempting her lips looked.

"There you two are," called Heather. "Are you going to join us for lunch?"

Heath found himself feeling disappointed that he and Gwen wouldn't get time alone together. "Sure, of course. If you'd like us to."

"Yes, come and sit," added Samantha, patting the empty chair beside her. "We're all taking a walk along the beach after lunch. What are you two doing?"

Heath and Gwen sat side by side. "Playing golf," Gwen replied. She released his hand and it felt empty and cold where it rested on the table.

He shook his head. What was wrong with him? He had to stop thinking that way. After this weekend, Gwen Alder wouldn't give him a second thought. He'd pay her first month's rent and they'd both move on with their lives. He didn't need the complication of feeling things for someone who didn't see him the same way.

"Golf? Ugh – boring," responded Samantha in her usual blunt fashion.

"I don't know. It might be romantic," stated Gwen, amidst oohs and ahhs from the women seated around her. She glanced over her shoulder at him and caught his eye, and he swore he saw a flash of something behind the sky-blue.

THE GOLF CLUB felt heavier in Gwen's hands than she'd thought it would. She practiced a swing while she waited for Heath to tee off. He'd seemed to find it inconceivable that she'd never played the game, but when she'd asked him when, pray tell, a working-class girl from Long Beach would have the chance to hit a small white ball around an exclusive country club, he'd shut his mouth. She'd smiled in satisfaction.

She watched as he swung the club high behind himself, then smoothly forward. The ball sailed down the center of the green and landed in the distance with a few short bounces on the neatly-clipped grass. He pivoted and smiled in her direction. "Your turn."

She thrust out her chin and walked toward the tee. She had this. She could do it. She'd always been pretty good at sports. Surely golf couldn't be any more difficult than basketball, and she'd won a championship in that sport – granted, it was when she was ten, but still. She stood in front of the tee and set her club beside the ball, her eyes locked on it.

Then she felt two hands slip down her arms from behind, and her skin goose-pimpled. "Like this," Heath said, his hands adjusting her grip on the club handle.

She nodded, momentarily unable to find her voice. Her legs felt like jelly as his body pressed against hers and he cradled her between his muscular arms.

"You have to set your feet about shoulder's width apart. Yep, just like that. Good."

She inhaled slowly, breathing in his musk and her head swam. "I think I've got it ..." She didn't have it – she could barely breathe.

"No, don't hold the club handle that way ... turn it like this. Good."

She focused down the causeway. There was a small hole down there somewhere. A flag shivered in the breeze. "Is that what I'm aiming for?" she asked, pointing toward the flag.

He let go and backed away. "That's it. Just wait until ..."

She swung as hard as she could, striking the ball and sending it flying off to the left. She watched it go, her mouth forming an O as it sailed toward a golf cart bouncing over the green. "Oh no ..."

"... until that party moves out of the way, is what I was going to say," finished Heath, his hands clenched at his sides. "Ball!" he shouted.

By then, two men had begun climbing out of the cart. They looked up and scrambled back in, just before the ball ricocheted off the roof with a *thwack!* Gwen grimaced, covering her eyes with her hands, then peered up at Heath between parted fingers. "Sorry."

He put his hands on his hips and cocked his head to one side. "Nice shot, though."

She waved to the men, now peeking warily out of the cart. They waved back, shaking their heads.

Heath sighed. "You do know that's Dad and Uncle Dave down there, right?"

She covered her mouth with one hand. "No!"

"Yep. Good work." He chuckled and set off toward where her ball had landed, waving his hand over his head to the other pair.

She rolled her eyes and groaned as she chased after him. Just great. She'd almost killed Heath's father and uncle. She was off to a great start. "Sorry, Graham," she said when she drew close.

Graham rested the edge of his putter against his ball, knocked it gently into the hole, then turned her way and laughed. "Never mind. You know this is *our* green? Yours is over that way."

She grimaced. "I know. I'm so sorry – I've never played before."

He shook his head. "I guess Heath will have to teach you some of the finer points of golfing ... so you don't maim anyone." All the men laughed at that.

Her cheeks flamed. "Again, I'm so sorry. I'm just glad no one was hurt."

"All's well that ends well," Uncle Dave replied, tapping his fingers to his forehead in a mock salute.

She smiled. "Thank you for being so understanding."

Graham faced Heath. "Now don't forget the rehearsal dinner tonight, son."

Heath nodded. "Thanks for the reminder, Dad. We'll be there."

"And maybe you could sit beside your mother and I this time? We'd love to hear more about you and Gwen." Graham walked away to get his ball.

When he was out of earshot, Heath turned to face

Gwen. "He wants to hear all about us at dinner tonight."

"Mm, I heard."

"What are we going to say? You told that ridiculous story about how we met. What else is there?"

"My guess is they'll want to know how you proposed."

He frowned and rubbed his chin. "Should we brainstorm ideas?"

Gwen chuckled. "No, this one is all yours."

8

GWEN SPUN TO THE RIGHT, THEN TO THE LEFT, admiring the way the red dress hugged her figure. She'd never worn anything like it before and felt a little exposed. But with a small black shrug around her shoulders she also felt elegant, and it brought a shy smile to her face.

When she opened the door of her room, Heath stood with his fist poised to knock again. His mouth hung open and his eyes widened.

"Hi," she said.

His hand fell to his side and he swallowed. "Hi."

"Ready to go?"

He seemed to have lost his voice, and it made her skin tingle. "Is that one of the dresses I bought you?" he finally asked, almost choking on the words.

She nodded, her cheeks flaming.

"Wow. Um ... I'm not sure if the bride will be quite as taken with it as I am, but ... wow."

She threw her head back and laughed. "Don't worry, I'm wearing something much more subtle to the wedding tomorrow. But I figured you'd want me to dress elegantly for the rehearsal dinner ... it's not too much, is it?"

He shook his head and offered her his arm. "No, I'm just teasing. It's absolutely perfect. I almost didn't recognize you."

Her eyes narrowed. She wasn't sure how to take that.

He seemed to sense her change of mood. "Not that you looked bad before," he stammered. "It's just that you usually look like the pretty girl next door, but ... sheesh. I'm really bad at this, aren't I? Let me start over ... you look beautiful. As always."

She giggled. "Thank you, boss. You look pretty good yourself." He wore a tuxedo perfectly fitted to his lithe frame. His hair was slicked back in waves away from his face. The way he'd tripped over his words was endearing. There were so many things about him she'd assumed and been wrong about.

This time, they were leaving the resort. A series of long black limousines waited in the curved driveway outside the front doors. Gwen and Heath climbed into one with his parents, Samantha, Brett and another man. Long upholstered bench seats ran down both sides of the vehicle and across the back. Gwen sat on one side, smoothed her skirt around her legs and leaned against Heath's shoulder, lacing her fingers through his. It was strange, but the action felt completely natural, and he seemed more accustomed to her touch as well.

"Gwen, I'd like you to meet my brother, Daniel Montgomery," said Heath, indicating the man seated across from her. He looked younger than Heath, with hazel eyes instead of blue, but the same dark wavy hair.

She held out a hand toward him. "Daniel, how nice to meet you."

"Daniel, this is my fiancée Gwen Alder."

Daniel's eyes widened as he shook Gwen's hand and glanced at his brother in confusion. "Pleased to meet you." His eyes narrowed and eyebrows arched at Heath.

Heath shook his head and shot a look at Graham and Arlene, who were involved in conversation.

Daniel frowned and cocked his head. "Engaged, huh? How about that? I'm happy for you, bro."

"Glad you made it in time for the rehearsal," added Heath, changing the subject of conversation. "I thought you might miss the whole thing."

"Yeah, well, my boss is a real ..."

"Would you look at the time?" interrupted Heath, with an exaggerated shake of his wrist, making his watch rattle. "I think we're going to be a little late."

Gwen watched the exchange with interest and a half-smile. "So, Daniel – do you work with Heath?"

He laughed and nodded. "Yep. He's my boss, I guess you could say. He likes to remind me of it often enough."

Heath chortled. "Come on, I've got to do something to keep you in line."

"Yes, sir!" Daniel offered his brother a mock salute, but his eyes sparkled.

"Sounds like you have fun together," she added, glancing back and forth between them.

"Eh, he's okay – urk!" Daniel responded, just as

Heath switched sides and got his brother in a headlock.

"Hey!" barked Arlene in a voice Gwen hadn't heard before. "Don't make me come over there and separate you boys."

Both boys separated, hair mussed, and stared at their mother. Heath returned to Gwen's side.

Gwen's eyes widened. "Whoa, I thought your mother was a lamb," she whispered.

"More like a lioness," he mumbled. "You should've seen her when we were kids. When she called us in for supper, she could yell all the way to the property line where the river was. I could even hear her if I was underwater." He laughed and Daniel joined him, the brothers sharing a knowing look.

Gwen smiled. This was a family she enjoyed being a part of – if only for a few days.

THE LIMOUSINE PULLED up in front of a large restaurant with *Salty's* written in cursive neon above a covered entryway. They made their way to the back of the building where a private porch had been set up for the dinner. The bride and groom were already there, along with a few other family members.

Gwen gasped as she looked around – it was like walking into a fairy tale. Round tables dotted the porch and fairy lights were hung around the outside and across the ceiling. The place settings were all in white with crystal glasses, and white flowers were mixed with vibrant greenery. White organza was hung from the ceiling, illuminated by the tiny yellow lights. "It's beautiful," she whispered.

Heath tightened his grip on her hand. She was glad he hadn't let go. She liked holding onto him more than she should, given their *relationship* would only last one more day, two at most. The thought tied a knot in her stomach. Breaking up would be hard to do – it might be a fake relationship, and the breakup would be no more real than their engagement was, but her gut still roiled whenever she thought about it.

Heath led her to their seats beside Graham and Arlene. She lowered herself into the chair and was glad to see Heath's Nana across from her. She waved.

Nana waved back. "How lovely you look!" she said loudly.

Her cheeks colored. "Thank you," she mouthed.

It was noisy in the room as the family, bridal party and friends of the bride and groom filed in. Finally everyone took their places and the wait staff began to bring out the food. They were interrupted in their conversations between each course for speeches and toasts.

Gwen found herself having more fun than she'd had in a long time. She'd thought being around the Montgomerys would be awkward and stiff. They were rich and privileged; she was poor and had to fight for every opportunity, every promotion, every penny. Yet she found them warm, welcoming and relaxed.

Just thinking about it made her throat tighten and tears spring to her eyes. She ducked her head, not wanting anyone to see. What was wrong with her? Maybe she was just homesick. It had been a difficult few years and she missed her folks, her friends, even missed Long Beach. But she could've gone back there after the divorce – why hadn't she?

Well ... because her family was nothing like this. Her mother would've blamed her for the divorce and asked why she didn't make things right with Ed, just as she did over the phone every time Gwen called her. Her stepfather would've ignored her, his eyes flitting back and forth until she moved out of the way of the TV that played constantly in the background. Her friends had all moved on with their lives. And she hadn't wanted to face them – she didn't want to go home a failure.

She dabbed her eyes with her napkin, then set it in her lap again.

"You okay?" asked Heath, his hand on her shoulder.

Just a single touch sent her nerves into a frenzy. "I'll be fine."

"What is it?"

"I just miss my family – and I don't. It's complicated."

He smiled. "Family usually is. We love them, but ..."

"... We can't live with them," she finished for him.

He chuckled. "Sometimes, that is very true."

She felt a tap on her other shoulder and turned to find Nana sitting beside her. She took Gwen's hands in hers, squeezing them tight. "Did I ever tell you about how Heath's grandfather and I met?"

Gwen shook her head. "No, you didn't." She loved hearing other people's stories.

"I was a dancer in a chorus line at a theatre in New York City ..."

Heath interrupted. "You were a dancer, Nana?"

She frowned, her forehead wrinkling. "Yes, my darling boy. Don't interrupt. Now Herb – that's Heath's grandfather – came to see the show. He was only in town for a few days on business and he thought he'd go to Broadway for a lark. Well, there I was, and he said I was the most beautiful woman he'd ever seen."

Her eyes grew dreamy and she stared off into the distance. "He was handsome, my Herb. And we fell in love, just like that." Her eyes fixed on Gwen's face, then traveled to Heath's and back again. "Don't let anyone tell you you can't fall in love that way. You can and it can be the most wonderful thing in the world. I'm so happy the two of you are getting married. It gives me something to look forward to." She stood, patted Gwen on the shoulder and turned to walk toward another table.

Gwen smiled down at her own hands, then met Heath's gaze, his eyes full of dark intensity. "Gwen ... I."

There was a shout and a crash. Gwen leaped to her feet, her heart in her throat. Nana had fallen over and lay still on the porch. She ran to Nana's side and bent over her. "Call an ambulance!" she shouted.

Heath was beside her in a moment, checking Nana's pulse. "Sam, where's Sam?" he shouted, glancing about the room. Gwen saw his sister hurrying toward them. "She's breathing," his voice was thick with emotion. "Nana, can you hear me?"

She groaned and rolled onto her back. "I feel a bit dizzy, dear ..."

~

GWEN'S EYES FELL SHUT, then bounced open again. She leaned back against the cold, sterile hospital wall and sighed. They'd been there for two hours already and still hadn't heard a thing. Heath's parents were in the room with Nana, but the rest of them were stranded in the waiting room.

Heath sat in a chair close by, his head in his hands. She walked over and sat beside him, resting a hand on his shoulder. "She'll be fine."

He glanced up at her and grimaced. "I hope so."

Graham and Arlene walked into the waiting room side by side with red-rimmed eyes. Graham cleared his throat and spoke to the group. "She's going to be okay."

There were sighs of relief all around. Gwen put her hand into Heath's and squeezed it.

"She's just had a bit too much excitement. You can all head back to the resort. They're going to keep her overnight just to monitor her vitals and make sure she didn't hurt herself. But she wanted me to tell you to have fun and don't miss out on a beautiful evening on her account."

A few of the family chuckled at that as everyone stood, stretched, yawned and began to make their way out to the parking lot. Heath walked over to his parents, one hand in his pocket, the other still clutching Gwen's. "Is that all?"

Daniel joined them, his eyes bloodshot. Graham glanced at Arlene, then faced his sons. "No. Nana didn't want us to tell everyone just yet – she wants them to enjoy the wedding. But you two should know, she's really sick."

Heath took a quick breath. "How sick?"

"Lymphoma – they found it last month. It's treatable, so don't jump to any conclusions, but the chemo has made her a bit woozy."

Daniel ran his hands through his hair and walked to the other side of the room.

Heath pulled Gwen a little closer, and she rested her cheek against his arm. She didn't know what to say, but could tell he was suffering over the news. All she could do was be there and hope that it helped.

HEATH SHIFTED gears and the truck lurched forward, the engine revving.

"Go easy, son," Graham scolded. "We won't make it over that hill if you give it too much gas."

"I know, Dad." He gritted his teeth and tried again. This time the truck topped the rise and continued down the muddy track, following Newton's four-wheel-drive. The groom had requested a four-wheeler outing rather than a bachelor party, and Heath had been glad to oblige. He loved getting out into the countryside, and the challenge of keeping a vehicle on the track and not getting bogged down usually piqued his competitive instincts.

But today, his mind was elsewhere. Nana had come home from the hospital early that morning. He'd heard her chastising the orderlies who wheeled her down the hallway. She'd been adamant she could

walk to her own room, but they hadn't allowed it. He
smiled at the memory.

"Take it back to second, Heath." His dad held onto
the dash with one hand, his knuckles white.

Heath rolled his eyes. "Dad, you can relax. I've
done this before."

"I still don't know why Newton chose to do this.
On the day of his wedding, no less. He could get hurt,
or stuck out here. What then?"

Heath chuckled. "Maybe that's what he wants."

Dad studied him through narrowed eyes. "What
do you mean?"

"I mean, maybe he doesn't want to get hitched
after all. He could be getting cold feet and this
would make a great excuse for not showing up to
the wedding – *I couldn't, dear, I was stuck in a
mudhole.* Suddenly he's off the hook." He laughed
and turned the steering wheel to avoid an enormous
pothole.

Dad gripped the dash a little tighter. "Is that what
you think of marriage, son?"

Heath took a slow breath. "No, Dad, of course not.
I was just making a joke."

"Because if it is, perhaps we need to have a little
talk. You're engaged, and I think maybe it's all moving
a little fast for you."

Heath sighed. "Really, Dad, I'm fine. I was just
having fun ..."

"I mean, we hardly know this girl. We don't know
her motives. Why would a pretty girl like Gwen make
such an impetuous decision and agree to marry
someone she barely knows? I think you should be a
little more suspicious and a little less trusting, son."

He blinked and grabbed his seatbelt with his free hand as the truck lurched to the right.

Heath's jaw clenched and his nostrils flared. His father always thought people were coming after their money. He could understand that – when you had money, there were so many who wanted it. But a lifetime of building his legacy had left his father cynical and wary. "Are you insinuating that she's only marrying me for my money, Dad?"

"I don't know, son."

"Because if you are, I can assure you that's not the case."

"How can you be so sure?"

Heath shook his head, angry that he had to explain himself. Angry that he had to defend Gwen when she'd done nothing to deserve it. Angry that even after running the man's company for him, his dad still didn't completely trust him. "Because she doesn't know how much money we have."

"What do you mean? You're engaged! She flew here on the jet with you. You're a Montgomery. Everyone knows us. Have you even met her family? Do you know anything about them? For all you know, they could behind this whole thing, encouraging her to come after you ..."

"I don't understand you, Dad." He could feel his blood pressure rising as frustration pulsed through his veins. "All this time, you've been on my case about getting married. You want me to settle down, have a family, so you can trust me with the business. Well, you're getting what you've always wanted – I'm engaged – and you're still not happy. You want to know what I think?"

"What?"

"I think you don't want to hand over the reins, so you're coming up with excuses to keep from doing it. Do you want me to be CEO or not, Dad? Just tell me, because I'm sick of all the games."

His Dad rubbed his eyes and exhaled slowly. "Of course I want you to be CEO."

"Do you trust me?"

"Yes, son, you know I do."

"Then make the announcement. Tell everyone this week when we get back to Billings, that I'm the new CEO. Step aside. If you don't want to, don't and I'll move on. I'll find something else to do. I want to make you proud, carry on your legacy, but only if that's what *you* want. If you don't, just tell me." He pulled the truck to a halt, rested both hands on the steering wheel and stared at his father.

"I'll do it," Dad said.

"Yes?"

"Yes. This week, I'll make the announcement." Dad smiled weakly.

"Only if you're sure. I don't want to force your hand – I just feel as if you're holding back because you don't believe in me."

"It's not that, son. It's hard for me to let go is all. I've built this company from the ground up over many years. Taking a step back is difficult."

"Then don't. But whatever you decide to do, please be honest with me about it."

Dad nodded and frowned. "You're a good son, Heath, and a good man. I trust you and I believe in you ... and it's time. Your mother's been asking me to retire for years now – if I changed my mind now and stayed on as CEO, she'd probably go traveling without me." He chuckled. "I will announce it this week."

Heath's throat constricted and he swallowed the lump that'd formed there. "Thanks, Dad. It means a lot to me. Don't think of it as leaving the company – you'll still be around, and I'll always value your input."

"I know. Come on, then, let's get moving. They're leaving us behind." Graham cleared his throat and waved a hand at the taillights disappearing over the rise ahead of them as Newton's SUV pulled away.

Heath stepped on the accelerator and followed the narrow trail through a thicket of Pacific dogwoods, their small white flowers forming an arch over the muddy track.

It was finally going to happen – he'd be CEO. Their ploy had worked. And once he was CEO, his father wouldn't think twice about his love life. Sure, he might be disappointed when Heath called of the engagement, though given his worries about Gwen's ulterior motives, maybe not. But he knew his father wouldn't change his mind about the promotion, not after it was announced to the entire company. All he and Gwen had to do was wait until after the announcement and they'd be home free.

A twinge of guilt flashed through him. He hated lying to his parents this way, but what other choice did he have? He hadn't dated anyone since Chantelle – or wanted to – and his father wasn't going to accept that he'd given up the bachelor lifestyle to stay home and watch documentaries on IFC or host a Bible study group in his living room. So he was doing what he had to. And one day they'd all laugh about it together.

He pulled to a stop behind Newton's vehicle, and Daniel jogged toward him as he and his father climbed out. They were at the top of a cliff looking over the ocean, and gulls circled overhead, their calls echoing across the water. He set his hands on his hips to survey the beautiful scenery and smiled at Dan.

Dan, though, wasn't smiling. "Hey, I haven't had a chance to talk to you ..."

Heath raised his eyebrows. "Uh-huh?"

Dan leaned close. "What's going on?" he whispered. "Is Gwen that waitress from the diner?"

Heath chuckled. "I was wondering when you'd ask me about that."

"I see you every single day. I know you haven't been dating anyone. So how are you suddenly engaged to a woman we've just met?"

Heath rubbed his chin and fixed his brother with a steely gaze. "You can't tell anyone."

Dan nodded, eyes narrowed.

"I'm paying her to pretend to be my fiancée."

Dan's eyes widened and he took a step back. "What?!"

"I know, it sounds ridiculous, but it's working – Dad just told me in the car that he'd announce me as CEO next week. After all this time waiting and him constantly nagging me to settle down and get married to prove I'm serious about the job – like that proves anything – he's finally going to take the 'acting' off my title."

Dan studied him, his nostrils flaring. "You're pretending to be engaged ... to get the promotion?"

Heath nodded, his cheeks flaming. Hearing it spoken made him all the more aware of just how crazy the whole plan was.

Dan shook his head. "Well, I'm glad it's working out for you. But you know you're gonna break Mom's heart, not to mention Nana's."

"I know, I know." Heath took a quick breath. "I admit I didn't think that part through very well. And now I don't know what to do about it."

Dan suddenly grinned. "She's a nice girl. Cute, too."

Heath's eyes rolled. "Yeah, she is. But don't get any ideas – it's a business transaction, nothing more."

"How on Earth did you get a girl like Gwen to agree to do it?"

"She's in a bit of a pinch right now – she needed the money."

"Well, if you ask me, you should hold onto her. You say she's been pretending, but I see the way she looks at you – that's something you can't fake." Dan walked away.

Heath watched him, his brow furrowed. He inhaled deeply and his gaze wandered over the cliff top, the circling gulls and the deep blue of the water down below. He wished Gwen were there with him now – she'd love the view. And his heart ached at the thought.

9

Gwen stretched out on the bed and put her cell phone to her ear. It rang, then Diana answered with a sing-song "Hel-lo?"

"Diana, it's Gwen."

"Oh, Gwen – how's the wedding? Are you having a wonderful time? I bet you are. Oregon ... wow. I'm so jealous."

Gwen chuckled. "It's pretty amazing here. I've never been to a wedding like this before – everything is so decadent compared to what I'm used to."

"Enjoy yourself. Everything here is just fine ... oh, I do have a couple of messages for you. Hold on ..." She could hear papers being shuffled. "... okay. The first one is from a Lisa Connelly – she says she has some resources for you, come see her Monday after the staff meeting and she'll get those to you."

"Oh, thanks. That's my new boss."

"And the second message is from an Ed Alder – I guess he must be related, huh? Anyway, he said to call him back as soon as you get the message. That's all he said – kind of a gruff guy."

Gwen shivered and rolled onto her back to stare at the ceiling. How had Ed gotten her new home number? Regardless, he was still coming after her about money she didn't have and didn't owe him. When would he finally leave her alone?

"Oh, and Gwen?"

"Yeah?"

"The rent is due Wednesday, so if you could get your first month's to me before then, I'd really appreciate it."

Gwen swallowed hard. "Yeah, of course. Thanks, Diana. I'll be home late tonight, so if you're asleep I'll see you in the morning."

She ended the call and laid still, her hands over her eyes. At least she had her rent covered, as soon as they got back to Billings and Heath paid her. She could manage rent, but things would be tight until her first paycheck from the school. Now if only Ed would get off her case – and preferably get a life. She sat up with a groan and reached for her swimsuit. Maybe a dip would help clear her head.

Downstairs at the pool, she dove into the cold water, letting the shock of it against her warm skin distract her from her whirling thoughts.

The feelings growing deep inside were ones she recognized, and they scared her. She was getting too attached to Heath – even now her mind strayed to him. She pictured him dressed in that tux, then in the cowboy hat and jeans he'd worn that first day, and her heart seized. She couldn't let herself feel things for him – it would only lead to heartbreak for her. She'd fallen for Ed too quickly and look how that had turned out. He hadn't been the man she'd thought he was.

But Heath was different, wasn't he?

She shook her head, clearing the water from her ears, and rested her arms on the side of the pool, kicking gently in the water. She was there for a reason – to get her rent paid and the recommendation letter. That was all. She'd already decided she would stay away from men. Yet now here she was mooning over someone who didn't think of her as a girlfriend, just as a convenient way to fool his family. Did she really want to get involved with someone like that?

Gwen's mind answered with *no*. But convincing her heart was another matter.

Later, stretched out on a poolside lounge, she skimmed a book on her Kindle but couldn't focus on the words. Normally she'd be immersed into the story, but today she couldn't concentrate.

The pool gate opened and Heath walked in, casually handsome in chinos, a button-down blue shirt, and a Stetson in contrast to the preppy clothes. She couldn't help smiling. "Good morning," she said, setting her Kindle down on the towel beside her.

He removed his sunglasses and looked her over. She was suddenly very aware that she was dressed only in a skimpy bikini. "Almost afternoon," he teased with a half-smile. "Enjoying yourself?"

She nodded and pulled a dress over her head. "I am, actually. It's been nice to relax for a little while."

"I thought you might like to come to lunch."

She stood and reached for her purse. "That sounds great – I'm starved, actually. Being lazy really works up an appetite." She chuckled and fell into step beside him as they headed for the elevator.

"I wish you could've come with me this morning. It was pretty spectacular."

"Oh?"

"Yeah, Oregon is really beautiful."

She nodded. "So's Montana."

He grinned. "You think you could settle there?"

"Where, in Montana?" A wave of butterflies jetted through her stomach.

"Yeah, in Montana."

"I guess so. I'm starting my new job tomorrow, so I'd say I'm pretty settled."

They stopped in front of the elevator doors and he pressed the button, then met her eyes. "I mean long-term."

"Oh, I don't know. Maybe."

"But your family is in California, right? You wouldn't mind being away from them?"

Where was he going with this? Her head buzzed and grew light. "Mom's in Arizona with my stepdad. Dad's passed. I've been away from Long Beach for years now and don't have any plans to move back there. I miss it sometimes, of course, but I think a visit is about all I could manage these days." She couldn't imagine moving back – it would be tantamount to giving up.

He nodded, looking pleased.

They stepped into the elevator, and she used her towel to dry her dripping hair so it wouldn't soak the floor. When the doors closed, he took her hands. "Gwen, I've been thinking ...."

She interrupted him, her heart racing. "Look,

Heath – everything's going the way you planned, right?"

He nodded, his brow furrowed.

"So let's just stick to the plan. You get the promotion, I get my money, we break up and go on with our lives. Okay?"

He released her hands and stepped away, his face drawn. "Sure, Gwen. That's fine with me."

Pain ripped through her heart. "I'm sorry, Heath …"

He smiled palely. "Nothing to be sorry about. That's what we agreed to."

Gwen stepped off the elevator first and hurried toward her hotel room, Heath close behind. Everything was working out just the way they'd wanted it to. She'd be able to pay her rent, and with her new job starting the next day her life was on track for the new beginning she'd longed for. So why did it hurt so much?

"EVERYONE SHOULD WEAR red lipstick at some time in their life, or they're just missing out on all the fun." Nana leaned forward in her salon chair and peered at her reflection in the mirror as she smeared lipstick in a wobbly line across her thin lips.

Gwen smiled. "Can I help you with that, Nana?"

Nana nodded and handed her the tube. Carefully Gwen finished the application, then moved aside so Nana could see the end result. "Much better, thank you, dear. Now where are my glasses?"

Gwen chuckled as Arlene reached over and slid

Nana's spectacles off the top of her head and back onto her nose.

"Oh dear, there they are. Don't worry, my darling, you'll be forgetting everything yourself before too much longer."

Arlene huffed. "Graham's already that way."

Nana's eyebrows arched. "Really? Hmmm ... must take after his father. I was still sharp as a tack at his age. So, Gwen dear, do tell – when are you and Heath going to hold your engagement party?"

Her heart plummeted. "Engagement party?"

Arlene pulled her chair closer to Gwen's. Her hair was curled tightly on rollers beneath a scarf to hold them in place. "You must have an engagement party. Everyone will be expecting it and we'd just love to celebrate the two of you."

Gwen's eyes widened. "Well, we haven't talked about it ..."

"Oh please, just say yes. I'll arrange the whole thing – you won't have to lift a finger. I've been waiting so long for Heath to find someone. Well, for any of my children to, but Heath is the oldest. And now that he's found you, we have to cherish every single moment of this special time."

Gwen swallowed and tugged at the collar of her dress, which suddenly seemed too tight. "Yes?" she whispered hesitantly.

Arlene clapped her hands and grinned. "Oh, wonderful! I'm so happy!"

Nana smiled and reached for a magazine to flip through. "Don't burst a blood vessel, Arlene dear." She winked at Gwen.

Arlene's smiled faded. "I won't, Nana. It's just a happy occasion and I'm excited about it."

Nana's eyes rolled. "It is wonderful, my dear. And of course, you're welcome to hold it at my place as long as I don't have to clean up. I'm getting too old for that sort of thing."

Arlene frowned. "I was thinking of our place, actually. What do you say, Gwen?"

"That would be lovely. Where do you and Graham live?"

"Over near Butte. It's not so far from Billings – I'm sure your friends won't mind making the trip. We have a big ranch outside of town, perfect for events like this."

Gwen nodded. She felt as though things were spinning out of control. Just when she'd begun to think life might land and she could make sense of it all, here it went again. And this time, she suspected that it might end in a *crash* landing.

THE SEA-BLUE DRESS shone in the sunlight slanting through the hotel room blinds. Gwen took a long slow breath and reached for a matching clutch she'd bought with the dress. This time she wore flats – less danger of toppling over when she walked. It was time for the wedding, the event the entire weekend had been building toward. She couldn't be more nervous.

She heard a knock at the door and hurried over, fixing her earrings into place as she went. Heath was standing there in a black tuxedo with a white vest, shirt and bowtie. His eyes sparkled and he held up an arm for her to take. "You look stunning once again," he said, leaning close.

Gwen could feel his breath on her cheek. Her heart pounded. "Thank you."

IN THE DRESSING ROOM, Heath glanced at his watch again. It was time for the wedding to start, but where was the groom? He'd spent the morning with Newton and the other groomsmen, but now that the moment for him to pledge his life to another had finally arrived, he was absent. And no one else seemed to notice. The rest of the groomsmen were sipping whisky, chatting away, generally oblivious to the roomful of people waiting next door in the resort's wedding chapel.

The door flew open and Newton burst in, his eyes wide. "Okay, let's do this thing."

Heath sighed in relief and hurried over to fix Newton's crooked tie and tidy his disheveled hair. "Where have you been?" he hissed, studying his cousin's face.

"What, am I late or something?"

Heath raised an eyebrow. "Don't worry about it. But let's just try to get through this without any incid ... wait. Have you been drinking?"

Newton giggled. "Mmmmaybe. Am I in trouble, Mr. Montgomery?"

Heath set his hands on his hips and growled. "Just ... hold it together. Do you think you can do that?"

Newton threw his arms around Heath and pulled him into an embrace that squeezed the breath from his lungs. "I love you, cousin. You've always been like a brother to me."

Heath chuckled and patted his back. "You too, Newt. I'm real happy for you. Congratulations."

"You're always there for me ..."

Heath coughed. "You too, buddy. I can't breathe."

"Oh." Newton released him.

Heath took a deep breath. "Okay, come on. I just hope your bride isn't ticked. We're supposed to be in there waiting for her."

"You think she's mad?" asked Newton, his eyes widening.

"Hopefully she's still fixing her hair. You know how ladies are."

Newton laughed and threw his arm around Heath's shoulders as they walked toward the chapel. "She's *sooo* beautiful, man. I don't deserve her, y'know?"

Heath nodded. "I know what you mean."

AT THE RECEPTION, Heath watched Gwen weave through the crowd to the head table. The speeches were done and the wedding party had dispersed, mostly to the dance floor. Her eyes shone as she smiled at him and he swallowed, crossing his arms to keep from reaching out for her. "Beautiful wedding," she said with a laugh. "You were a very handsome groomsman, Heath."

His heart skipped a beat. She'd said his name instead of calling him *boss*, or *sir*, or something equally obnoxious. It was no good. He'd tried to convince himself against starting something with her. When he'd broached the subject, she'd shut him down so fast his head was still spinning. But he couldn't help how he felt. They were flying home right after the reception, and he wouldn't have to see her again. That was the key, since being with her only made him want her more. "Thank you. I'm just glad it's over, to be honest."

She arched an eyebrow. "Not a fan of weddings?"

"They're fine. But there's a lot going on back at the office and I should be there."

"Oh." She stared at her hands.

"And Dad and I had an argument this morning."

"I'm sorry."

He frowned and ran his fingers through his hair. "It's fine – I won the argument. He's announcing this week that he's making me CEO. I tried to tell you earlier by the pool ..."

Her eyes widened. "Oh, that's great news – congratulations!"

He nodded. But he found he couldn't feel good about it. "So let me know when you're ready to go. The jet is at the airport waiting and we'll be home this evening." He chewed on his lower lip.

"Thanks." She didn't sound thrilled either. Probably because she'd been having such a good time, and tomorrow she'd be at work. He'd noticed she'd taken advantage of the pool and spa, and she sure got along well with the women in his family. It didn't have anything to do with him ... did it?

"I'll make sure to get the money and the letter to you as soon as I can." He wanted to reassure her. Or maybe reassure himself that he'd see her again, if only once. But she didn't look reassured, just nodded and turned away. "Though, um, I don't think we should head off until we've at least had a dance," he added on impulse.

Her eyes widened and her smile reappeared. "That would be great."

He took her hand and led her to the dance floor, where the band was playing a quiet instrumental rendition of Jewel's "You Were Meant for Me." He pulled her close and tucked their joined hands under his chin as his other arm encircled her back. She looked up at him, her eyes clouded. What was holding her back? She seemed to feel the connection they had. Perhaps she figured they didn't know each other well enough. Or maybe it was the divorce – did she still have feelings for her ex? Or was she too wounded to trust her heart?

"This is nice," she murmured.

"It is nice. I'm glad we did this ... Don't get me wrong, I feel bad we fooled everyone. But I'm not sorry I asked you to come along this weekend. It's been great."

She nodded. "It has. Surprisingly great."

"Why surprising?"

She laughed. "You're very curious, aren't you Heath Montgomery?"

"True. I want to know everything. Or at least as much as possible."

She laughed harder. "Okay, okay ... the reason it's surprising is that I really didn't think we had a lot in common when I agreed to this. So ..." Her cheeks flushed.

"And now you think we do have things in

common?" He grinned and pressed his body against hers.

Her lips pursed, but her eyes twinkled. "I guess you could say that."

"I think so too."

There was a tap on his shoulder. Dan stood behind him, hands deep in his pockets. "Can I cut in?"

Heath stepped aside and tried to swallow his annoyance. "Sure."

Dan took Gwen in his arms and expertly led her around the dance floor. She laughed as he dipped her backward, and when he held her close they spoke in hushed tones. Heath stood at the dance floor's edge, arms crossed. What was with Dan? Couldn't he see Heath was finally connecting with Gwen? Or maybe he had – butting in and taking over was what he'd done since they were kids.

He scowled and took a deep breath. No need to get upset about it, he'd just go back to the head table and have a drink with Newton and his new bride. But when he got there, it looked as if Newton had already drunk enough for the evening. "Newt, can I get you a cup of coffee? Some water, maybe?"

"Gin 'n tonic," slurred Newton, his smile crooked.

"Uh- huh." Heath glanced back at the dance floor and watched his brother spin Gwen out and back. She threw her head back and laughed, a hearty laugh he hadn't heard from her before. His nostrils flared.

Newton chuckled. "You're jealoush."

Heath frowned. "What are you talking about?"

"Dan's dancin' with your fiancée and you're jealous. I don't know why, since she said she'll marry *you*. But sometimes that just isn't enough, I guessh."

He spun a glass in front of him, staring at it morosely.

"Are you okay?"

Newton grinned. "I'm fan-tashtic."

"Where's Heather?"

He turned his head from side to side. "I dunno. Hm ... guessh I should go find her." He stood and stumbled off across the room.

Heath rolled his eyes before returning them to his brother and *fiancée*. He didn't have to stand for it – after all, she was his date. He strode to the dance floor and tapped his brother on the shoulder. "My turn."

Dan glanced back in surprise. "Sure ..." But before he could finish, Heath had Gwen in his arms and had whisked her away.

Gwen caught her breath, then chuckled. "What was *that* about?"

"I'm sure I don't know what you mean –" Heath felt another tap on his shoulder and scowled. "What?"

Daniel stood there, cell phone in hand. "You feeling all right, Heath? Adam's on the phone for you."

"Sorry. Thanks." He grabbed the phone, gave Gwen an apologetic shrug, and headed off the dance floor and out to the patio, leaning against the railing. "Adam, this is Heath. Is something wrong?"

"Hey, Heath. Sorry for interrupting your weekend – again – but I thought you'd want to know I figured out what the issues were with the financial reports. I'm not sure of all the details yet, but I know where the errors are. We can talk more about it when you get back to the office."

"Thanks, Adam. I'll be in tomorrow – we can

discuss it then. But I'm glad we're getting to the bottom of it. Some of those figures just don't make sense."

"I know. I've got when and how – now I just need to find out why and who. There's some money missing, but I can't say any more just yet."

Heath concluded the call and looked out over the golf course. There was a chill in the air, but it wasn't cold enough to be uncomfortable. A few dim lights lit the course, and couples strolled hand in hand beneath the porch along a footpath that led to the resort's small nightclub. He sighed and rubbed his eyes. He was anxious to get back to Billings, but at the same time, he didn't want to leave. Leaving would mean his pretend engagement would end. And he wasn't ready for them to break up. Not just yet.

10

GWEN LEANED HER HEAD BACK ON THE SEAT AS THE JET engines hummed beneath her, making everything gently vibrate. She closed her eyes and exhaled slowly. It'd been a big weekend, and though she'd taken plenty of opportunities to relax, for some reason she was bone-tired.

Heath sat down beside her and handed her a mineral water. "Thank you again for coming with me this weekend."

She took a sip. "Thanks for asking me. And for paying my rent." She chuckled and flashed a grin.

"You're welcome."

By the time the limousine carried them from the jet center in Billings to Gwen's apartment, she was almost asleep. She'd changed into jeans and sandals after the reception, carrying her gowns in a brand-new garment bag Heath had insisted on buying her. Would she ever get a chance to wear them again, considering her work life revolved around crayons and reading groups and her personal life involved the occasional trip to a café or the movies? Still, she smiled at the memory of how she'd looked in them, and the reflection of that in Heath's eyes.

Heath walked her to her door, pulling her luggage on its bumpy plastic wheels behind him. He leaned against the door frame as she quietly unlocked the door. She glanced up at him, her heart pounding and her palms damp with sweat. "So I guess this is goodbye."

"For now. I'll see you tomorrow."

"Oh?"

"After work, I'll get you the money and the letter you need."

"Oh, right. Thanks."

"Hope it goes well at school tomorrow." He was stalling, she could tell. What was going on in his head?

"Thanks. You too, with the whole CEO announcement and stuff."

He raised an eyebrow. "Yeah, thanks." He leaned closer. Was he going to kiss her? She pursed her lips and her pulse accelerated, making her head buzz.

He pulled away. "All right ... well, see you tomorrow, then."

She bit her lower lip and frowned. "Okay. Bye." Why didn't he kiss her? Well, maybe because she'd told him she didn't want anything more than a business relationship between them? Still, she'd been sure he was about to try. But now he was trotting away as though he didn't have a care in the world. She sighed and rubbed her face with both hands.

Inside, she found Diana bouncing around the

kitchen to Taylor Swift. "Why are you still awake? It's after midnight."

Diana grabbed her by the hand and spun her around. "I made margaritas!"

"Okaaay. Well, I'll pass, since I already had champagne at the wedding. But you have fun." Gwen pulled her luggage into her room and set it down, then headed to the kitchen for a glass of milk and a chocolate chip cookie. She'd finally gotten to the store, and she always kept her cookie jar well-stocked.

"I have news," continued Diana, sipping her drink.

"Oh?" Gwen poured hers and selected a cookie from the jar.

Diana walked over and shoved her hand under Gwen's nose. "I'm engaged!"

Gwen's eyes crossed on the gigantic blue rock on Diana's ring finger. "Wow! That's some ring."

"I know. Isn't it beautiful?" Diana threw her arms around Gwen, almost knocking the glass of milk over. "I'm enga-a-a-aged!"

Gwen laughed and patted her on the back. "Congratulations. I'm really happy for you."

Diana stepped back and her face fell. "I'm sorry, I'm not upsetting you with all this engagement talk, am I? I know how much your divorce hurt …"

Gwen shook her head. "No, no, of course not. It's fine. I'm glad you're happy."

Diana took another sip of her margarita. "You know, you'll find someone one day."

"I know … actually, I didn't want to rain on your parade, but Heath and I are engaged as well." She raised her voice in an attempt to match Diana's excitement, but instead sounded like a cheerleader.

Diana's eyes widened. "What? Really? Wow, that was fast. Oh, we're going to be brides together – that's so fantastic! I was wondering what you'd do once I got married, since you just moved in, but now I won't have to worry about it because you'll be moving into Heath's place. Oh, that's great!" She hugged Gwen again.

Gwen frowned against her shoulder. She hadn't thought of that. Once Diana was married, would she have to find somewhere new to live? She might not be able to rent this apartment on her own.

She pasted a smile to her face. "That's right. No reason to stress about it – we're both getting married. It'll be great."

"Now you *have* to drink a margarita with me, so we can toast!"

Gwen stifled a yawn. "Sure, okay." She could barely keep her eyes open, but she took the offered drink and raised it. "To us," she said.

"To us," echoed Diana with a smile. And they both drank. Even as Gwen wondered how she'd managed to get herself even deeper into this jam.

THE LUCKY DINER sign glowed yellow against the dark sky. Heath stepped out of his beat-up truck and loosened his tie. It had been a hard day at the office, putting out fires, managing staff issues and catching up on everything. He hadn't even had a chance to meet with Adam about the financial irregularities, though the CFO had said he was still working out the details. He patted his coat pocket, checking that the money and letter were still there, then headed inside.

He saw Gwen right away in a booth by the window. She smiled when she saw him. He kissed her cheek and slid into the booth opposite her, grinning back. Then pulled the envelope out of his pocket and set it on the table in front of her. "There you go."

"Thanks. You don't know how much it means to me. Really, you're a lifesaver."

He nodded. "Glad to help. How did school go today?"

She was about to answer when a waitress stopped by their booth, pencil poised above her pad. "Howdy, Gwen. Nice to see you." Gwen chatted with the waitress for a few moments, then ordered a cheeseburger, salad and milkshake. Heath placed his order and the waitress left them alone.

"School was great." Gwen played with the envelope. "I'm just so glad to be teaching again. Well, not actually teaching yet, but getting the classroom ready and meeting the other teachers ..." She sighed. "I just loved it. I can't wait for next week. Teaching is what I'm meant for. At least, that's what I think." Her cheeks flushed.

He smiled. "I'm sure you're a great teacher. I know I would've loved to be in your class – I would've had an enormous crush on you."

She laughed and rolled her eyes. "They're in third grade, I highly doubt you would've had a crush on me in the third grade."

"Oh, don't underestimate me," he joked. The waitress brought their orders and Heath took the top off his burger bun to add more ketchup.

"So I guess this is it," she mused.

"I guess." He took a bite of hamburger, his thoughts in a swirl. He didn't want that to be it. If they parted ways now, would he ever see her again? "Actually, I've been thinking about something."

"Yes?"

"Nana was so happy about our engagement, and she's going to be at the hospital every day this week getting treatment. I wondered if ... maybe we could postpone the breakup. Just until she's feeling better."

She frowned and sipped her lemonade. "So we'd stay engaged?"

"Just a bit longer. I don't want to upset her while she's feeling so bad." He cleared his throat. It *was* the truth – he didn't want to disappoint Nana. And it would also buy him some time, give them a chance to get to know each other better ... who knows?

She smiled. "Sure. Okay, I can do that."

Heath smiled back, suddenly feeling like a weight had been lifted from his shoulders.

ON HIS WAY home from the diner, he stopped in at Nana's house to check on her. She lay on the couch, flicking through channels on her widescreen TV. "Heath, dear – how lovely." She sat up and straightened her hair.

He kissed her cheek and sat down beside her. "How are you, Nana?"

"Oh, as well as can be expected. Nora – that's the live-in nurse your father hired today – is in the kitchen. She can get you a drink if you'd like."

Heath chuckled. "She's not your maid, Nana."

"Oh, she doesn't mind fetching things for me. What else does she have to do?"

He smiled. "Well, I'm glad you're okay. I'll check in on you again tomorrow on my way home from work."

"Thank you, dear. But why aren't you out with Gwen? The two of you are so sweet together. I'm just so excited you're getting married – the wedding will be beautiful."

He swallowed hard and nodded. "Yes, I guess so."

She pinched both his cheeks. "Oh, it will be. And maybe I'll even get some great-grand children before I go."

He sighed. "Don't talk like that, Nana. You're going to live a long time yet."

"No one knows how long they'll live, my boy. And I've had a good long life. But I would like to see you married and happy with a wife and children."

He half-smiled. "I know, Nana."

"So your mother and I are planning quite the engagement party, I hope you know. After the announcement, the two of you will be the talk of the town."

Heath nodded – he'd heard about that from Gwen. He wasn't sure how they would get out of that one.

～

THE NOISES of the office surrounded Heath the moment he stepped off the elevator. He'd gone for a ride around the ranch Tuesday morning on his favorite stock horse, Hilda. Her chestnut coat had gleamed in the early morning light, and his breath had been visible in the chill air. It had been relaxing, invigorating – just what he needed. But now, the sounds of printers whirring, phones ringing, voices engaged in urgent conversation all served to increase his heart rate. He smiled tightly at several employees who hurried by, then headed for his office.

He'd barely had a chance to sit when Adam poked his head in the door. "Good morning."

"Morning, Adam. Coffee?"

Adam shook his head. "First, can you come in my office for a moment? I have to show you something."

"Okay." He got up, followed Adam into his office and pulled up a chair. "What's up?"

"You know how we've been scouring the financial reports and I told you I'd found something?"

"Uh-huh." From the look on Adam's face, the news wasn't good. "Give it to me straight. What's going on in my company?"

"Someone's defrauding us."

His eyes widened. "Are you sure? I mean, you said some money was missing, but I assumed it was an accounting error or something."

"Yes, I'm sure. At first it was just a feeling, then I noticed a specific set of figures that didn't add up. So I've been looking through everything, and I mean everything, from the past five years. And I've found discrepancies here and there that by themselves might not mean a lot, but added together ... it's a half million dollars, Heath."

He coughed, as if choking on the revelation. "What?!"

Adam raised an eyebrow. "I'm sorry, Heath, but it's

true. Whoever's involved has stolen ..." He tapped a key on his laptop. "... by my count, $503,771.27. Give or take a nickel."

Heath sighed long and loud. "Do we know who?"

"I've found a trail that leads to *someone* – whether or not it's that person, I can't say for certain. I think we should turn over everything we've found to the police, but I wanted to talk to you about it first, get your read on things."

"Who?" Heath leaned forward, his elbows on his thighs and rubbed his face.

"Paula Weston."

"In Accounting? Wow." She'd made him a cake for his last birthday – chocolate with vanilla buttercream. It couldn't be Paula.

"As I said, neither of us is an investigator. Maybe someone's making it look like it's Paula and she's not even involved. I can't say for certain."

Heath nodded. "You're right. We should report this to the authorities. They'll be able to get to the bottom of it. Thanks for working on this, Adam. I can always count on you."

Adam nodded and frowned. "Happy to help. Sorry for being part of the cause."

"What? It's not your fault."

Adam's face fell. "Technically it is. I'm in charge of finance. How did I let something like this slip by?"

Heath sighed. "I don't know. We all missed it somehow. And it's really bad timing, with the handover from Dad coming up. You know who the board will blame ..."

Adam sighed. "I know. They're not convinced about you. Some of them wanted to open the CEO position up for external applications. But hopefully Graham will convince them you're the right person for the job."

"Unless the fraud lands at my door."

"You didn't know," Adam insisted. "You couldn't have known. It was my fault – I should've seen this a long time ago."

"But you trusted your staff."

"I trusted my staff, just the way you've trusted me. And I let you down."

Heath stood. "Don't worry, Adam. If it comes down to it, I'll take the heat. I don't want you getting the blame for something that happened on my watch. That's one of the joys of being the boss – everything is my fault." He walked back to his office.

Once he sat down, he began mentally kicking himself. If only he'd realized earlier what was going on. How had they missed a half-million-dollar theft? Well, there was nothing he could do about that now except report it and hope the police got to the bottom of things. Perhaps they'd even recover some of the money, if they were lucky.

There was no point telling either his father or the board about the fraud until they knew more – as soon as he shared this crisis with them, they'd want answers and right now he had none. Paula Weston? It was hard to imagine she'd acted alone, not with such a thorough cover-up that even his perfectionist CFO hadn't noticed the missing money. When the cops uncovered the truth, he'd tell his father and the board everything – and bear the brunt of their anger. He knew he'd be held to account – he was the one ultimately responsible for everything that happened within the company.

He leaned back in his chair with a sigh. He'd better handle things carefully from this point on or he could find himself in real trouble. He pressed the intercom button. "Judy?"

"Yes, Mr. Montgomery."

"Can you please grab me a coffee?"

"Yes, sir."

"Then bring your tablet in here. I need you to take care of some things, and you'll want to take notes."

11

GWEN SIGHED AND RAN A HAND THROUGH HER HAIR before flopping onto the couch. She was exhausted after teaching third grade for two weeks. With Lisa's help she'd found her way around the school and figured out most of what she had to do. The other teachers had given her a warm welcome, and the children were mostly sweet and eager to please. But it was still hard work.

She smiled as she flicked on the TV. Diana wasn't home yet, and she usually had about an hour or so to herself in the afternoons. She'd come to relish that time to decompress after the long day. She lay back on the couch and flipped through the channels, looking for something to watch.

But even as she landed on a murder mystery, her thoughts wandered. What was Heath doing at that moment? Likely working, since it was only 4 p.m. But she couldn't help thinking about him. She hadn't seen him since he gave her the money and the letter, and there was an ache in her chest every time she thought of him. She should just call him and ask how he was doing. After all, they hadn't broken up yet, not officially. It would make sense for her to call. And she wanted to know how Nana's treatment was going.

Perhaps she should just drop into the office to see him. If she called, he could answer her questions easily enough and they might not see one another. No, she should go and see him. It was exactly what a fiancée would do.

Gwen dropped the television remote into her lap and let her eyes drift shut. Tomorrow she'd go see him, ask him how he was doing, how Nana was coping with her treatments. Then, she'd feel better about things. And who knew - maybe she'd be able to concentrate on her own life instead of daydreaming about Heath Montgomery.

THE NEXT DAY AFTER SCHOOL, Gwen pulled into Montgomery Ranches' underground parking garage. She grimaced at the parking charges on the sign next to the ticket machine, then drove beneath the boom gate and inside. Maybe they would validate.

When the elevator doors dinged open, she glanced around wide-eyed. The office buzzed with activity. Staff hurried in every direction, all dressed in business suits with only the occasional pair of cowboy boots to give away the business's roots. She approached the reception desk, checking her hair with both hands and wishing she'd swung by her apartment to freshen up first.

"Good afternoon – how can I help you?" asked a petite blonde woman with enormous round glasses.

"Oh, hi. Um, I'm Gwen Alder and I wanted to see Heath Montgomery." Why did her voice sound so hoarse? She coughed to clear her throat.

The woman frowned imperceptibly as she clicked the mouse on her computer. "Do you have an appointment, Miss Alder?"

Gwen shook her head. "No, but ... he's a friend. He'll want to see me."

She looked skeptical. "I'll let him know you're here." She pressed a few buttons, then spoke into her headset. "Mr. Montgomery, there's a Gwen Alder at reception to see you ... oh! I didn't know ... yes, sir, I'll tell her." Now she smiled at Gwen, her eyes shining with a knowing glint. "He'll be down in just a moment, Miss Alder."

Gwen's heart skipped, and she took a quick breath and smoothed her pencil skirt with damp palms.

Heath appeared through a doorway, smiled and reached for her hand. She stumbled forward and embraced him awkwardly. He kissed her cheek, and the feel of his breath against her skin made her goose-pimple all over. "Gwen, I wasn't expecting to see you."

She arched an eyebrow. "Sorry, I should've called first. I'm sure you're busy."

"It's fine – come on through." He gestured toward the doorway, then followed her down a long hall, with offices on one side and cubicles filling a large open space on the other. Windows covered the far wall, and she could see directly into the building next door where office workers scurried around just as purposefully as they did there.

"Your offices are really great," she said, then winced, wanting to slap her forehead for her lame attempt at conversation.

"Thanks. We've been here about five years now, so it's definitely home."

"I thought you said you were in the ranching business. What are all these people doing?"

He chuckled. "We've diversified a bit. We have over a dozen ranches plus ancillary businesses related to ranching, and many of those are franchised as well. So we keep pretty busy."

She nodded, working hard not to gape at the size of the operation. She hadn't expected this. Obviously he was well off – the company jet had made that clear enough – but she hadn't realized just how big Montgomery Ranches was. And he was the CEO and heir. Her stomach twisted into knots. There was no way he'd be interested in a real relationship with her. Not that it stopped her from daydreaming.

She followed him into a large square office, and he shut the door behind them and offered her a seat. She sat, glancing around at the vibrant artwork that hung on two walls. One wall held a depiction of a bronco bucking as a cowboy held on tight; the opposite wall, a picture of the city of Billings. Behind his desk hung various business documents, accolades and awards. She swallowed hard and brushed her hair back. "It's good to see you, Heath."

He grinned. "You too. I'm glad you came in. I've been wondering about you ..."

"Oh?" Him too?

"Just wondering how you are, how your job's going, that sort of thing."

She smiled and inhaled slowly, trying to calm her fluttering heart. "I'm fine. Things are going well. I absolutely love my new job – the kids are adorable and we're settling into the school year pretty well. It took me a week to figure out the lunchtime schedules, where the nearest bathrooms are and where the children go for gym, music and library, but I think I've got it down now."

He laughed. "I'll bet it can be tricky at first."

She found herself keenly aware of how well his suit fitted his lithe physique, and wished she could come up with something witty to say. "How are things here?"

"Good. Actually, I don't think I've spoken to you since Dad retired and nominated me as the new CEO. The board approved it immediately and made the announcement. Now I'm just trying to settle into the role – well, I've had the role for years, but now I get to relax in it."

Her smile widened. "That's great. I'm really happy for you."

He nodded. "Thank you. I'm scrambling to get a few things under control, but that's business, I suppose."

"I'm sure you'll be fine. I should take you out to celebrate – let's have dinner somewhere." Where had that come from? No doubt he'd already have plans. She wiped her hands on her skirt again.

"Dinner? That would be really nice, actually. I'm basically finished for the day, or at least there's nothing that can't wait for tomorrow. We could go now."

Now? Gwen would kill to be able to go home,

shower and change into something pretty first. But her wrinkled blouse and skirt with sensible flats would just have to do. She nodded. "Great. Now is perfect."

GWEN LEANED against the door in Heath's old blue pickup, but its rattling rhythm was giving her a headache. She sighed and moved back against the headrest. Where should they eat? She'd just offered to take him to dinner but hadn't been paid yet, so she couldn't take him to the kind of restaurants he was used to patronizing. "How about the Lucky Diner?" she asked, squinting into the afternoon sun.

He grinned. "The Lucky Diner it is. Are you still working there?"

She shook her head. "Nope. But I probably will over Thanksgiving and Christmas breaks."

He raised an eyebrow. "Because the pay is so great?"

"Because I need the money." Her throat tightened. She hated having to admit that to anyone, especially Heath. Obviously he knew things were tight – she'd agreed to pretend to be his fiancée for rent money. But it was hard to open up and share just how bad things had gotten.

His eyes clouded with concern. "I can lend you some if you need more."

She shook her head and forced herself to sound light-hearted. "Oh no, thank you – I'm fine. I'll get paid soon and things will get better from there. At least that's the plan."

As he parked in the Lucky Diner's lot, he glanced her way several more times, his brow furrowed. She forced herself to look straight ahead. If he showed sympathy, she might just collapse in a puddle of tears. She had to hold herself together.

Inside, they sat in the same booth as the last time they were there. Gwen's mind flashed over the memory of their first encounter and her cheeks blazed at what she'd thought of him. A scruffy, cocky cowboy who hadn't showered in days – she hadn't wanted anything to do with him. But now ... she sighed and looked over the menu she knew by heart.

They ordered, and when the server took their menus she folded her hands in her lap to give them something to do other than fidget with the ketchup bottle in the middle of the table. She noted the pink of his cheeks and the way he smiled politely at the waitress. "Heath ... I wanted to talk to you about something. I ..."

"Hello, Heath Montgomery." A breezy voice interrupted and she looked up to see a perfectly primped blonde woman leaning on their table with two manicured hands.

Heath's eyes darkened and he looked distracted before focusing on the woman. "Chantelle. How nice to see you." He didn't sound like himself. "This is Gwen Adler. Gwen, this is Chantelle, an old ..."

"Girlfriend," Chantelle finished for him with a satisfied smirk.

"Pleased to meet you, Chantelle." Gwen offered her hand.

Chantelle eyed it with disdain before turning back to Heath and smiling coyly. "Actually, I can't stay. But I

saw your truck pull in here and I wanted to congratu-
late you."

"Oh?" Heath's smile faded.

"Yes. Imagine my surprise when your mother told
me you were engaged. I couldn't believe it – after all,
you said you weren't the marrying type. I thought she
must be mistaken ... Heath Montgomery engaged so
soon after we broke up ..."

Heath sighed and ran his hand through his hair.
"We broke up a long time ago, Chantelle. And I told
you I wasn't the type to marry *you* – we weren't suited
to each other ..."

Her eyes flashed. "Well, never mind – it's all in the
past." She glared at Gwen, her gaze dropping to where
Gwen had settled her hands on the table. She grinned
predatorily. "But I'd love to see your ring."

$\sim$

CHANTELLE STRODE for the diner door, almost hissing
as the bell rang overhead. She hated those bells.
Hated diners even more. Who would eat in such a
place? She'd always known Heath Montgomery
wasn't good enough for her. And to marry that plain
Jane in the flat sandals with her hair drooping around
her face. There was nothing special about her, that
much was clear.

A man pushed past her through the doorway, and
she spun on her Jimmy Choo stilettos to glare at his
retreating back. What was wrong with everyone? Was
she suddenly invisible? She stamped her foot angrily
against the ground and felt one of her heels buckle.
Just great! All she needed was to break a six-hundred-

dollar shoe. Now she'd have to hobble across the uneven lot to her car. With an angry grunt she bent to retrieve the heel, then stared at it in dismay.

She fought back the threatening tears. What was wrong with men? She was so careful about the ones she dated, yet they all eventually tossed her aside. She couldn't understand it – she worked so hard to take care of herself, to build up a network of friends in the right circles. She was educated, gave to charity and even volunteered occasionally ... or thought about it, at least.

She glared at Heath and his new fiancée through the tall window beside their booth and frowned. The man who'd pushed through the door and into the diner past her was standing at their booth, gesturing wildly. She could hear his raised voice through the glass. Who was he?

He stomped toward the door, and she pushed herself up against the wall to make way for him as he rushed by. Then Gwen ran past, caught up to him and grabbed his arm. He spun around to face her with a snarl. "What do you want?"

Chantelle felt exposed where she stood and scooted to the right until she was hidden in the crook of the wall. She leaned forward to peer around the edge. She could see them well enough and their voices hummed just above the rush-hour traffic.

"I should ask you the same. Why won't you understand?"

The man crossed his arms over his thick chest. "Oh, I understand – my wife's having dinner with another man. How could I not understand that?"

"Ex-wife," corrected Gwen. "How can it possibly

matter to you who I eat with? We're divorced! And what are you doing here, anyway? How did you find me?"

His cheeks colored. "I found out you worked here. What does it matter how …?"

Gwen clenched her fists at her sides. "You've got to stop this. Just leave me alone, Ed. We're through, we're divorced, I wish you all the best in life, but it's time for you to move on."

"Well, you've certainly moved on quick enough." For a big man, he sure pouted a lot. Chantelle suppressed a smirk. No wonder she dumped him.

"It's not what it looks like."

"Oh, it's not?"

"No. Heath and I are just friends."

"You and Mr. Business Suit in there are just friends? You think I'm that stupid? Well, let me tell you, I don't care if you marry him, but don't think that means I won't go for alimony. In fact, looks to me like you'll be able to afford a whole lot more. You cry poor, but I don't buy it." He grinned.

Chantelle's eyes widened. He was shaking her down! What a scumbag.

Gwen sighed and put her hands on her hips. "I'm not marrying him. We were just pretending to be engaged so he could get a promotion at work."

Ed's face turned red. "And what do you get out of it?"

She paused. "He paid first month's rent for my new apartment. Anyway, what does this have to do with you? I'm not marrying him, I'm not coming into any money, so you can just go home and forget about me."

He barked a laugh. "Aw, Gwen, you know I'm never gonna do that. Not while you still owe me." He turned and walked away.

"I don't owe you anything!" Gwen yelled as he walked away, still laughing. She growled and marched back into the diner.

Satisfied that she hadn't been seen, Chantelle wobbled on her one good heel across the lot to her Mustang. So Heath and Gwen were only pretending to be engaged? What a joke! She should've realized something was up the moment she laid eyes on Heath's fiancée. He wouldn't dump her only to propose to someone who looked like *that*. A last glance over her shoulder revealed Heath and Gwen in deep conversation, leaning forward across the table between them. Heath didn't look happy.

Chantelle smiled to herself and slid into her convertible. It was a beautiful evening. Maybe she'd ride home with the top down.

HEATH TAPPED the pen against his desk like a woodpecker, then sighed and set it down. He couldn't focus, couldn't stop thinking about Gwen and her exhusband. He'd known she was divorced, but hadn't expected him to show up while they were eating and berate her about alimony. Alimony? How on Earth would a primary-school teacher owe alimony? And what kind of man would seek it when he was perfectly capable of working? It didn't make sense.

And she wouldn't talk to him about it. He'd asked her point-blank what was going on and she'd assured him she was taking care of it. But what did that mean? Obviously she didn't have the best legal representation to help her out if she'd gotten into such a jam in the first place.

He stood and took a quick breath. Dan should be back from lunch by now – he'd just pop into his brother's office and ask him a quick legal question.

Sure enough, Dan was seated at his desk going over contracts they'd just signed with a breeder in Wyoming – Heath had approved the deal. "Dan, have you got a minute?" he asked, sliding into a chair.

Dan looked up with a grin and nodded. "Sure, big brother. What can I do for you?"

"I don't know if you knew this, but Gwen's divorced."

Dan opened his mouth to respond, thought better of it and closed it.

"Anyway, her ex is hounding her about alimony."

"Alimony?"

"Yeah, I thought it was strange as well."

"Do they have kids?"

Heath shook his head. "No."

"Okay. You want me to look into it for you?"

"Would you? It's just that he's giving her grief and I know she's struggling to make ends meet as it is. I think maybe she got a raw deal in her divorce settlement. But she won't talk about it ... what? I can tell you're dying to say something."

Dan chuckled. "Are you really still fake-engaged to her?"

Heath blushed. "Well, we didn't want to upset Nana."

"Uh-huh. That's all it is? Come on, Heath, you're

acting like this isn't a big deal, but it is. You're lying to everyone and now you're getting interested in her life. You like her and you're going to get hurt."

Heath rubbed his eyes and sighed. "I know."

"So end it. Or don't. But do something."

He stood and shoved his hands in his pockets. "So you'll look into her situation?"

"Sure. Just get me her lawyer's contact details and I'll give them a call."

"Will do." He headed for the door, then stopped. "And thanks, Dan."

Dan smiled. "What are little brothers for?"

Back in his own office, Heath stared at Gwen's name and number on his cell phone screen as his heart pounded. What should he do? He was in too deep emotionally. He knew Dan was right – he'd get hurt, his family would get hurt ... Gwen could be hurt. But all those would happen if he backed out, too. He sighed, jabbed the screen and heard her pick up on the first ring. "Gwen? It's Heath. Hey, can you text me your lawyer's details?"

Gwen's voice was bright. "Fran? Why?"

"Dan just wants to ask her a few questions. Oh, and can you call her to give permission for Dan to look into your divorce settlement as well?"

"Does he think he can help?"

"He does. But he'll have to talk to Fran first to get all the details."

"Okay. Thanks, Heath. You don't have to do this."

"I know, but I want to help. Oh, and Nana and Mom want to meet tomorrow to plan the engagement party. They've basically got it all worked out and just want to get our okay."

He heard her sharp intake of breath. "Sure. That sounds fun."

With a chuckle, he shook his head. "I know it's awkward, but as far as they know we're engaged."

"I just hope they haven't spent too much money yet."

He squeezed his eyes shut. "Knowing them, I'm sure they have. But hey, at least they're happy."

After he finished the call, he wondered if it was enough. Would these moments of joy cover the pain that'd come later when he and Gwen faked their break-up or, worse still, if Nana and Mom discovered their engagement was make-believe?

Heath sighed and rested his chin in his hand, studying the computer screen in front of him, but the numbers all jumbled together. He shook his head. He had to focus on work – it was the only thing that made sense anymore. Somehow he'd managed to turn the rest of his life into farce. He couldn't let the business suffer because of it.

12

HEATH PEERED THROUGH THE WINDOW INTO THE HOTEL lobby, but he couldn't see the restaurant from there and wasn't sure if Mom and Nana had arrived yet. Likely they were already holed up in a corner of the room plotting the biggest, most outrageous engagement party Billings society had ever seen.

He took a quick breath and walked through the door and across the marble floor. The elegant black-and-white decor of the Princeton Hotel was a familiar sight – the family and company had held many a function there over the years. Their high tea was one of his mother's favorite things to do on a weekend.

He found them quickly, seated at Mom's favorite table, one that looked out over the terrace. Gwen was there already, giving him a look that said, *where have you been?!* He simply nodded hello and sat.

She jumped up to kiss him softly, making his heart skip a beat. "Hi, pumpkin. You look nice."

He glanced down at his T-shirt and torn jeans,

shrugged, then set his Stetson on the table and kissed his mother on her cheek.

His mother's nostrils flared as she eyed his jeans. "Hon, I told you it was high tea at the Princeton, didn't I?"

He chuckled. "Yes, Mom, you did. But I have to put up with suits all week long. I want to be comfortable on the weekend."

"Well, I hope you don't dress like this to attend that church of yours." She arched an eyebrow.

He smiled. She always called it *that church of yours*. She didn't approve and she never missed an opportunity to make sure he knew when she didn't approve of something. "I do, Mom. Which is one of the reasons I love going there. They don't care how I dress."

She shook her head and made a tutting sound.

Gwen giggled, but quickly hid her smile behind a hand. "This looks delightful, Arlene – thank you so much for inviting me. I don't think I've ever had high tea before."

"It's so much fun, isn't it?" added Nana with a grin.

Heath leaned over to kiss Nana's cheek and squeezed her hand. "How are you feeling Nana?"

"As well as can be expected, dear. But let's talk about you young folk. That's a far more interesting subject."

He rested his hands on the table. "So does this mean I have to drink tea from one of these little flowery cups?" He lifted one in the air and tilted it from side to side. It was rimmed with gold and had pink rose buds all over. The handle felt as though it might break between his fingers at any moment. He set it down again, shaking his head.

Gwen laughed. "I'm really looking forward to seeing that. Perhaps you should raise your pinky finger in the air when you do it."

His mother rolled her eyes. "Could the two of you take this a little more seriously, please?"

Heath winked at Gwen, then chuckled. "Okay, Mom, what do you want to talk to us about?"

She pulled a day planner from her purse and laid it on the table. "Let's get the date of the engagement party set first, then we can go through all the details. Nana and I have come up with some ideas, but we want to make sure you're both on board."

While his mother talked over party plans, Heath's mind wandered. Gwen leaned forward, looked through flyers, sipped tea and nibbled at the finger food brought out on tiered plates. She wore casual clothes, fitted slacks and a blouse, but there was something different about her. She glowed. No longer the tired server at the Lucky Diner, the smudges under her eyes were gone, her eyes shone as she spoke. And she laughed a lot more. His heart raced and he thought about running his fingers through her hair, cupping her back, pulling her close and ...

"Heath?" His mother eyed him impatiently over the top of her glasses. "Where are you, off with the fairies? Please focus – we have to get these things finalized. After all, it's *your* engagement party. Anyone would think you had no interest in ..."

Her voice faded out again, and he nodded at what he thought were the appropriate times. She seemed pleased with his response. He settled back in his chair and linked his hands behind his head. The fact was, he wasn't particularly interested in the party. It was all a sham. He and Gwen planned to break up before it happened, so it didn't matter if they had roses or lilies.

He kept looking at Gwen, noticing how her hair fell like silk around her shoulders – the curls looked soft to the touch. The curve of her neck invited a kiss, but he bit his lip and crossed his legs instead.

She glanced up at him, a question in her eyes. Had he missed something? One look at his mother revealed he had. "Uh, yeah ... that's fine."

Mom nodded and continued her monologue, but Gwen kept her eyes on him, clearly suppressing a smile. "What are you doing?" she mouthed, a sparkle in her eyes.

He smiled, took her hand and laced his fingers through hers. A spark leaped from her skin to his and her eyes widened in surprise. He shrugged, then mouthed back, "What? We're engaged."

His mother didn't notice they weren't listening to her party-planning advice, but one look at Nana revealed they had *her* attention. She grinned and winked at them. Had she guessed the truth between them? Or was she just happy to see him "in love"?

Heath couldn't say what the future held. But in that moment, he had Gwen by his side, was holding her hand and was content. She might be gone from his life in only a few days, and he'd have to concoct another story to explain it to his family. The joy on his mother's face and twinkling in Nana's eyes would be replaced with grief, even anger. But for now, he could enjoy the moment. She was his, if only for a little while. And he hadn't felt so happy in a long time.

GWEN SPUN the curling iron like the lady in the YouTube video had, but it never seemed to work out the way it was supposed to. The woman in the video had produced large, soft curls falling around her shoulders. Gwen did the same and got her hair got stuck in the device. She yanked harder and smoke began to rise from her hair. Her eyes widened in alarm. "Umm ... Diana?" she called, pulling harder still. "Can you help me for a moment, please?!"

Diana hurried into the bathroom, her hair perfectly coiffed and her makeup done. Her eyebrows arched when she saw the fix Gwen was in, then deftly untwisted the curling iron and removed it from Gwen's hair. The piece of hair it had been attached to was singed into a tangle, and Diana giggled. "What on Earth were you trying to do?"

"Big soft curls, the type that bounce on your shoulders," Gwen grumbled. She ran a brush through her hair, which only turned the tangle into a frizz.

"Uh-huh. Well, I've got to go to work. Please try not to burn the place down while I'm gone." She laughed as she walked away, then called back over her shoulder. "Oh, and we should go on a double date tonight! Evan wants to meet Heath, since we're all headed for the altar. What do you think?"

Gwen's heart sank. "Uh, sure. Sounds like a great idea." She set the curling iron on the vanity and rubbed her face. Their lies were becoming a more tangled mess than her hair – she wasn't sure how much longer she could stand it. Why did she have to lie to her roommate as well? But when Diana was boasting about how she'd found someone else and that Gwen would one day, she'd wanted to say something to show Diana she didn't need her pity. And now she'd have to tell Heath what she'd done, and she had a feeling he wouldn't be very happy about it.

She wandered to the kitchen, pulled her cell phone from its charger and dialed. "Hi, Heath, it's Gwen. Just wondering what you're doing tonight ..."

Much to Gwen's surprise, Heath agreed to the plan. When she told him what she'd said to Diana, he just laughed and said something about "the more the merrier." Afterward, she frowned as she dropped the phone into her purse. He'd sounded less serious than usual, almost happy. She wondered what had happened to loosen him up so much.

AFTER WORK, Gwen made another attempt at curling her hair, with no better results. By the time Heath arrived at the apartment, she'd managed to put on makeup and the red dress from their weekend away. Diana let him in and she heard the introductions as Diana's fiancé Evan met Heath. Their conversation turned to what they'd each been doing and she heard Heath mention a Bible study group. She'd have to remember to ask him about that. She hadn't found a church in Billings yet and she missed attending.

She entered the kitchen and found Heath deep in conversation with Evan about boats. Apparently Evan was a serious sailor. "Hi."

Heath turned to face her and his eyes widened. "Wow – you look amazing."

Evan's eyes widened as well, and Diana's narrowed

when she noticed his response. "We're not going to a ball," she said.

"Oh, am I overdressed?" She knew she should've worn something else, but she didn't have anything nice other than the gowns Heath had bought her in Oregon.

"Not at all," replied Evan, getting a punch on the arm from Diana for his trouble.

"No, you look perfect," added Heath.

She smiled. "Let's go, then."

The restaurant was a trendy tapas bar on Broadway. Heath knew the restaurant staff and guided them to a table even though the place was full, his hand resting on the small of Gwen's back. She missed his touch when he removed it to pull her chair out for her.

"Wow, this place is great," she said, looking around the darkened room at the simple decor and fashionable crowd. The steady beat of modern jazz pumped through the restaurant, a backdrop to the buzz and hum of conversation as patrons leaned over small round tables, heads together, to be nearer each other.

"So Heath, Gwen tells me you're a cowboy," Diana said.

He grinned and raised his pants leg to reveal cowboy boots. "She's not lying."

"I'll go get us drinks," said Evan, eyeing the packed bar. "What does everyone want?"

Gwen asked for soda and lime, and studied Heath's face while Evan took the others' drink orders. He hadn't shaved that morning, and the stubble on his chin and cheeks made him look more mature and rugged. Her skin tingled, thinking about the way his hand felt when he'd held hers during high tea.

"If you're really a cowboy, wouldn't you live on a ranch and ride horses and stuff like that?" Diana asked, crossing her legs.

Heath raised an eyebrow. "I do live on a ranch just outside of town, and I ride as often as I can. But I also work in an office – is that allowed? Or do I have to hand in my cowboy card?" His eyes twinkled as he winked at Gwen. She smiled and swallowed a giggle.

"How do we know that's true? Have you seen his ranch, Gwen?"

Gwen's eyes widened. What was Diana doing? "Uh ...well ..."

"She's coming out tomorrow after school," interrupted Heath. He took Gwen's hand firmly in his. "I'm taking her riding. Isn't that right, Gwen?"

Gwen nodded, smiling in relief. "That's right."

Diana frowned. "Now that *is* a surprise."

Evan returned with the drinks and set them on the table. "What did I miss?" he asked.

"Nothing – let's dance," replied Diana with a last glance at Gwen.

Gwen's smile froze. Diana was clearly suspicious about her relationship with Heath, and couldn't put her finger on why, so she was probing. With good reason – all these weeks of engagement and yet they hardly saw each other. Even when they did, their affection wasn't particularly convincing. Oh, how she wished this charade could be over ...

Except that she didn't want it to end. Or maybe she just didn't want it to be a charade.

HEATH slung the rope around the fence paling and tightened the knot. Princess, a bay mare with black socks, nudged him with her nose, looking for a pat. He scratched her nose lovingly and pushed the long forelock from her eyes. "You be good today, girl. I've got someone special coming to ride you – no funny business, okay?"

She tossed her head as if in agreement. He chuckled, threw a fresh handful of hay in front of her and left the barn. He'd taken a day away from the office to get on top of things around the ranch, and he hadn't felt this good in a long time. He loved the land, even offering to help his foreman ride the property lines to get a feel for how things were going. It often frustrated him how little time he got for ranch work these days, but that's how things would be now he was CEO of Montgomery Ranches.

He slung a lasso over his shoulder and headed for the yard where the yearlings were milling around. There were a few he wanted to single out for auction the next day. He stood on the lowest rail to watch them for a few minutes, his eyes checking the curve of each neck, the strength of long legs. He was pleased with the past year's crop of stock horses. He ran a hand over the stubble on his chin. Mom hated it when he didn't shave, but he enjoyed the small rebellion.

He heard a car crunching up the ranch's long gravel driveway and turned his head to see who it was. Most of the ranch hands had already left for the day after an early start, and he wasn't expecting Gwen

until later. His heart sank when he saw the red
Mustang convertible approaching – Chantelle. What
was she doing here? He frowned and stepped down
from the fence.

She pulled up beside the ranch house and
stepped out of the car, showing off her long legs and
red flats. He rolled his eyes, tipped his Stetson back
and watched her approach. "Good afternoon," he said
as neutrally as he could.

She smiled, her teeth gleaming white between
very pink lips. "Heath, how lovely to see you."

"It is a surprise," he added, hoping she'd just get
to the point and tell him what she was up to. It wasn't
likely.

She crossed her tanned arms and turned to lean
back against the fence. "So how're you doing?"

"Fine, thanks. You?"

"Fine."

There was a moment of silence, and he studied
her face for some sign of what she might be thinking.
When they'd dated, she'd come to the ranch about
every other day, but not once since they broke up.
What had prompted her to drive all the way out
there now?

"Is the ranch going well –"

"Chantelle, what's on your mind?"

She sighed. "I just wanted to see you, to talk to
you. I thought you might be ... lonely."

He chuckled. "Lonely? Chantelle, you know I'm
engaged. I told you that – you even met my fiancée at
the diner."

She rested a hand on his arm and looked at him

with wide eyes and a smirk. "But I also know she's not really your fiancée."

His heart seized. How could she know that? "What?"

She laughed haughtily. "Oh, Heath, do you think I'm so simple that I couldn't figure it out? I know what love looks like, Heath, and you and Gwen aren't in love."

"I don't think you can tell that from one meeting ..."

"Plus I heard her talking to her ex-husband about it."

He swallowed. It suddenly made sense.

"So I know you're feeling lonely, Heath, when you start pretending to be in a relationship. That's a cry for help." She began to massage his arm.

He stared at her hand a moment, then pushed it away, his brow furrowed. "I'm fine, Chantelle. And what I do with my life is none of your affair."

She stared up at him with wide puppy-dog eyes "Heath, I really think we should give it another try. You didn't give us a chance before, not a real one, and I think we could be good together. Don't you?"

Heath's stomach churned. "No."

She pulled back as if he'd slapped her. "What?"

"Chantelle, I'm sorry, but I don't think it would ever work between us. I don't feel that way about you, and you know why we aren't suited. We spoke about it when we broke up."

She shook her head. "No, not really. You said something about church and God and how you didn't think I was good enough for you. But ..."

"No. That's not what I said at all. You know I'm a Christian."

"Yes, I know."

"You and I want different things. My faith's important to me. You and I aren't on the same page about that, and about a lot of other things. It wouldn't work."

Her nostrils flared. "I'm sorry you feel that way," she snarled. "You'll be sorry, Heath. I'm the best thing that ever happened to you and you'll regret the day you turned your back on me." She spun on her heel and marched to her car, her nose in the air.

Heath watched her go, rolling his eyes as she sprayed gravel in her departure. He'd dodged a bullet when he broke up with her, he knew that now. But her knowing about his and Gwen's ruse ... that was disturbing. Chantelle could make trouble with that knowledge, and she was the kind to do just that.

13

HEATH POURED COFFEE INTO A MUG, SET IT ON THE counter and stirred a teaspoon of sugar into it. He shook his head – hopefully it was the last time he'd see Chantelle, but he didn't expect to be that lucky. The women in his life would be the death of him – Chantelle, Mom, Nana, Gwen. At least he had fun with Gwen. He strolled out the porch, sat on the top step and took a sip of coffee. The sun was low in the sky, sending golden light across the pastures and highlighting the dull red of the barn.

What was he going to do? Chantelle knew the truth, while Mom and Nana were planning the mother of all engagement parties. Work was busy enough to require his whole attention, especially with the police investigating the embezzlement. There were too many distractions in his personal life – it was all he could do to stay on top of things.

Another car rolled up the drive – thankfully, a silver Corolla with a ding in the front bumper. He stood, sipped his coffee again, then walked out to meet Gwen.

She climbed from the car and embraced him, then backed away, smiling shyly. He looked her over appreciatively – dark jeans, a blue blouse that brought out the color of her eyes, her hair pulled into a youthful ponytail.

"I guess we don't have to kiss, since there's no one here to see us." She laughed.

He smiled in response. "No, but we can if you'd like to."

She blushed. "Well, I'd really like a tour of the ranch."

He nodded. "I'll just put my mug back in the kitchen and we'll go for a ride."

She arched an eyebrow. "So we're really going to ride horses? I've never ridden a horse before – I don't know if I can."

"You'll be fine, I promise. I've picked a sweetheart of a horse for you."

GWEN WATCHED Heath stride into the ranch house, then return with his hat and without the coffee cup. His faded jeans clung to his muscular thighs and a white T-shirt accentuated the curves of his arms. She swallowed hard as butterflies flurried in her stomach.

"Ready?" he asked.

She nodded. "As I'll ever be." She followed him into the barn.

He stopped in front of a stall where a dark brown horse with a black mane and tail munched hay. "This is Princess – she'll be your tour guide today." He chuckled and stroked the horse's head.

Gwen lifted a hand and ran it down Princess' forehead. Her coat was soft, and she nibbled at Gwen's arm with gentle lips, making her laugh. "That tickles." She stepped aside as Heath put a bridle over the horse's head and pushed the bit into her mouth. He saddled her and handed the reins to Gwen, who fed Princess a straw of hay at a time, getting used to the whole idea.

He emerged from deeper in the barn leading a golden horse with a light mane and much taller. "What would you like to see first?"

She pointed to a long structure in the distance. "What's that building?"

"That's the bunkhouse. It's a bit old-fashioned, but a few of the staff choose to live on the property. I go over and join them for a game of cards every now and then."

She nodded. "Sounds like fun." She looked at the two-story ranch house, casting a long shadow in the afternoon light. She'd hate to live on her own in a place that big, especially at night. "Do you live alone?"

"I do. I have a housekeeper, but she's not live-in."

"Isn't it lonely?"

He laughed and rubbed his chin. "That's the second time I've been called lonely today. Am I wearing a sign?"

"Sorry, I didn't mean to be rude."

"No, it's fine." He stared at the house with darkened eyes. "You're right, it's kind of empty. I hope it won't always be, but ..." He shrugged.

"You want to get married someday?"

He smiled. "Is that a proposal?"

Her heart skipped. "No, just ... curious. You seem very content on your own."

"Here, let me help you mount up. Put your foot in the stirrup, then push yourself up ... that's the way." Heath assisted her into the saddle, and she stared at the ground in dismay. It was a long way down. She gathered up the reins and held tight.

Heath climbed into his own saddle and tipped his hat. "You're right. I am content on my own, always have been. But I don't want to stay that way forever. I'd like to get married, have a family, fill that big empty house up one day." He urged his horse forward, and Princess followed obediently without Gwen having to do a thing.

Heath took her around the ranch and showed her the small herd of longhorns they kept in the south pasture. The rest of the stock were breed horses, and she laughed at the antics of the foals, now a few months old, as they frolicked and played in the setting sun. She enjoyed every minute of it, until Princess got bored and cantered back to the barn without warning, scaring the life out of her. The horse ducked inside, stopped suddenly and dropped her head to eat more hay. Gwen held on for dear life, her heart slamming against her ribs and sweat trickling down her spine.

Heath's horse cantered into the barn behind her. "You okay?" he called.

She nodded and exhaled sharply. "I'm fine. That was fun."

He laughed. "I'm glad. She's a good horse, but she loves to run home."

Gwen rubbed Princess' neck, then climbed carefully down from her back. Her legs and rear end ached as she hobbled over toward Heath, who was unsaddling his horse.

"You hurting?" he asked.

She nodded. "A little."

"Look, Gwen ... there's something I wanted to talk to you about."

"Yes?" She frowned. "What is it?"

"Tomorrow's Saturday and we're having a family picnic down at Holloway Falls. I think it would be a good opportunity for us to break up."

Her stomach flipped. "What? You want us to break up now? But what about the engagement party? What about Nana?" And what about her? She didn't want to break up yet. They'd just had such a good time together, riding around the ranch. What made him change his mind about their fake engagement? Was it something she said?s

"I think it's time. Nana will only be hurt more if we carry on longer. And Mom too. I don't regret it, don't get me wrong – I've really enjoyed getting to know you. But I did it so Dad would make me CEO, and he's done that. You did it for the money, and you've taken care of that. So there's really no reason to keep it up. I think it's just going to make things worse. Besides ..."

She forced a smile. "Besides what?"

"Do you remember Chantelle? The woman who came into the diner ...?"

"Your ex-girlfriend?"

He nodded and lifted the saddle from Princess' back, setting it on the ground with a grunt. "She overheard you and Ed talking. She knows we're not really engaged. And I don't know what she'll do with that information."

Gwen rolled her eyes. "Oh, for Heaven's sake ..."

"I know. It's just time, don't you think? We can break up at the picnic, have a big blow-up and everyone will see it. That way we can avoid all the questions and just get it over with."

She sighed, then nodded. "Okay. Let's break up." She handed him Princess' reins and walked out of the barn.

Leaning against the fence railing, she watched him brush Princess down and lead her to a gate in the fence. He let her out into the adjacent pasture along with the horse he'd ridden, and both trotted toward the herd grazing in the distance, heads raised high. He turned toward her, his face a mask. What was he thinking? Were his thoughts in as much turmoil as hers?

Her throat tightened and she stared at the ground. "Well, I should head back to town. Thanks for showing me around."

He walked over to her, his hands in his pockets. "No problem. So I'll pick you up at the apartment – say, eleven o'clock?"

"Okay, great." She turned on her heel and walked away. "See you then."

She got to her car as tears blurred her vision. She didn't want him to see her cry, but couldn't hold it back any longer. She pulled the door open, slid onto the seat and choked on a sob. Why was she so upset? It wasn't as though they were really breaking up, since they weren't really engaged in the first place. It was all pretend ...

Gwen gulped as the tears ran down her face unchecked. Maybe her heart had stopped pretending.

GWEN PULLED the covers over her head, then the pillow. Diana's music in the living room was giving her a headache. All she wanted to do was sleep, but everything was working against her. Sunlight slanted between the gaps in the curtains, birds called loudly outside the window, children squealed and shouted in the playground next door to the apartment complex. And on top of that, Diana was blasting Katy Perry.

"Just let me sleep," she groaned as she rolled onto her side. She didn't want to get out of bed. She was tired. The past few months had been a rollercoaster of emotions, one crisis after another, and she needed some time to recover.

Diana opened the door a crack and stuck her head in with a grin. "Are you getting up today?"

"Nope."

"It's nearly ten o'clock. I've never seen you sleep so late. And don't you have that Montgomery family picnic today?"

Gwen moaned and squeezed her eyes shut. "Yeah ... I'll be up soon."

She heard Diana pad across the room and felt the bed move as she sat at the end. "Are you okay? Did something happen?"

Gwen shook her head and cleared her aching throat. "Nothing happened. I'm just tired."

Diana stood and headed for the door. "All right.

Let me know if I can get you anything." The door shut quietly.

Gwen gritted her teeth. It was kind of Diana to ask after her and to care, but all she wanted right now was to be left alone. Which wasn't possible, since Heath would be picking her up in an hour. She sighed and sat up on the bed, figuring she might as well get on with it. Today was their last hurrah – a big argument at the picnic, and they'd no longer be engaged. Not that they'd ever really been engaged, she mused, staring at her empty ring finger.

But it still felt like the end of something – and like a hand was squeezing her heart.

When Heath arrived, her mood hadn't improved. She'd slapped on shorts, a blouse and cowgirl boots – an homage to Heath's ranch and what might have been – then completed the ensemble with an old straw hat that wouldn't stay on her head in a stiff breeze. She'd run a brush through her hair, but didn't bother with makeup. Why should she? All they intended to do was split up – why bother looking good for that? She opened the door and glared at him.

His eyes widened and he cocked his head to one side. "Good ... morning?"

"Eh." She turned her back and headed for her bedroom to collect her purse.

He followed her, clearly still confused. "Uh ... is everything okay?"

"Everything's fine. Bye, Diana," she called over her shoulder as she left. Her voice was cold, abrupt, but she knew that if she said more the lump in her throat might break free and the tears would fall. She had to pull herself together – she'd never make it through a family picnic this way.

Heath opened the door of his truck for her and she climbed in. The vinyl seat felt cool against her skin and she leaned back against the head rest. *Breathe. Just breathe. You can do this.*

He climbed into the driver's seat, looking concerned. "Gwen ..."

She faced him. "Why do we have to break up in front of everyone?"

"Well ... I just thought it'd make things easier ..."

"Easier for who?"

"I guess for my family. They'd see we aren't suited. Otherwise, they'd probably try to get us back together – play matchmaker, you know. I don't want Mom or Nana to be hurt more than they have to."

She sighed and faced forward again. "Okay."

He started the truck, still studying her with a frown. "Did something happen?"

"No. I'm fine. Let's just get this over with."

His eyes narrowed and he scratched his chin, then pulled away from the curb. "You're gonna have to tell me what's wrong."

"Why? Who cares? We won't see each other again after today. We're not friends. You don't care about me ... so what does it matter?" Her words started out angry, but ended in despair.

He sighed. "Is that what you think, that I don't care about you? That's not true."

"Ugh – fine, don't worry about it. We'll do this and everything will go back to the way it was. Just don't expect me to like it."

He didn't reply, just kept his eyes on the road, his

knuckles white against the steering wheel. She reached for the radio dial and turned it on, flicking through channels until she found a Taylor Swift tune, then turned it up and sang along to the words:

So THIS IS *me swallowing my pride*
　Standing in front of you saying I'm sorry for that night
　And I go back to December all the time
　It turns out freedom ain't nothing but missing you ...

"Is THERE ANYTHING ELSE ON?" he asked, exasperated. He turned the dial until rock music blared, then leaned back against his seat with a sigh.

Why had the lyrics to that song bothered him so much? She couldn't help smiling in satisfaction. Maybe he was struggling with them breaking up as well? Though you'd never know it by his stone face. She grimaced and crossed her legs. "So we should probably figure out what we're going to say –"

A loud bang! The truck fishtailed, then swerved left, almost crossing the median. A car traveling toward them honked loudly as it passed. Gwen grabbed the dash with both hands, her heart pounding.

Before long, Heath got control of the vehicle and pulled onto the shoulder. He turned off the engine and climbed out, his brow furrowed. "Blown tire," he growled, slamming the truck door shut and glaring at her.

Gwen fumed – why was he angry at *her* now? She hadn't punctured his tire! This whole situation was his fault – he was the one who'd wanted her to be his fake fiancée. It had been his idea to keep the relationship going even after he was made CEO. He was the one who'd said they should break up at the picnic. All she'd gotten out of it was a letter, an envelope of money and an extra heartbreak she didn't need. Her pulse jackhammering, she opened her door and climbed out.

He was on her side of the truck, bent over examining a very flat right rear tire. "Are you upset at me about something?" she asked, hands on her hips.

He glanced at her, his eyes dark. "No, of course not."

"Because none of this is my fault ..."

He straightened and glared at her. "You mean it's all mine."

"Yes, actually."

He raised an eyebrow and headed for the truck bed. "Fine, you're right, it's all my fault. Can you help me change this tire?"

Her fists clenched. He wasn't taking her seriously. She knew she was acting irrationally, but didn't care. He'd gotten her into this situation, this relationship. He'd made her care about him. He was too kind, funny, smart and handsome – it *was* all his fault. How was she supposed to stay detached? He could've kept her at arm's length.

He carried a jack and tire iron back to the torn tire, and she glared at him again. "Fine, I'll help. But this conversation isn't over."

"Got it." He set the jack beneath the truck, pumped it up until the tire was off the ground, then removed the lugnuts with the tire iron. She stood beside him with her arms crossed. She'd never changed a tire before, and though he'd asked for help he seemed to have everything under control. She glanced around, wondering what else might need doing, then locked on his flexing biceps and just stared.

"I'm sorry you're ..." He grunted as he shifted another lugnut. "... hurt. I didn't mean to hurt you. I hope you know that."

Her throat tightened. "Well, that's good to know," she replied sarcastically. She leaned forward to watch him work, letting the scent of sweat, soap and after-shave relax her a little. She took another step closer.

He leaned back and they collided. "Ow!" he cried, grabbing his hand.

"Oh no! I'm sorry – what happened?" She leaned over to look at his hand ... and her forehead whacked against his, sending her reeling. "Ouch!" She landed on her back on the sidewalk, her head in a clump of weeds growing from a crack in the pavement.

He grunted and rubbed his forehead with his undamaged hand. "What are you trying to do, kill me?" he grumbled. He stood up and headed for the cab, but tripped over the tire iron, stumbled sideways and sat down, hard, right next to her. "Oof!"

Her head throbbed and her eyes smarted with tears. "No, I'm not trying to kill you." She sat up, a little woozy from the fall. "Ugh ... but don't give me ideas. What happened?"

"Lost my grip on the tire iron ... banged my hand on the asphalt ... oh, great, I'm bleeding ..."

"Oh, I'm sorry ... urgh." She lay back down, resting her head in the weeds.

Heath's face hovered over hers. "Are you okay?"

She nodded. "A bit dizzy ..."

He pushed a strand of hair out of her eyes. She focused on his eyes, and time stood still. His blue eyes were intense as they met hers. Her heart beat a staccato rhythm in her chest.

"Are you sure?"

She nodded again. "Heath, I'm sorry. I didn't mean to ..."

His lips closed over hers, stifling her apology. She put her arms around his shoulders, her fingers winding through the thick dark hair at his collar. Her skin burned at his touch. What were they doing? This was crazy – they were supposed to be breaking up!

But in that moment the only place Gwen wanted to be was in his arms.

14

HEATH OFFERED GWEN A HAND AND HELPED HER TO her feet. Her cheeks were flushed and there was leaf litter all over her blonde hair. She held her straw hat in one hand and her eyes flitted toward his for a moment, then away again.

They'd kissed. And not just any kiss, but the most amazing, intense kiss of his entire life. It was as if all the weeks they'd known each other, every momentary caress, every peck on the cheek, had built toward it.

After the kiss, they sat side by side on the curb, talking and laughing – about anything and nothing. Conversation simply flowed in a way he'd never experienced. It was simple, easy, right. There was something so warm about Gwen – being with her felt like home. He hardly noticed the busy street in front of them. They'd even talked about church – and she'd asked if she could go with him.

He knew they should discuss their relationship. But they didn't. It was like they had an unspoken agreement to avoid the subject. What was there to discuss? They couldn't go back in time, couldn't change what they'd done. So they talked about other things instead.

"I guess we missed the picnic," Gwen finally said, brushing grass off her legs.

He shook his head. "I don't know – we should head out there and see. I would call, but I know what Mom will say. And I still have to finish changing this tire. I was about to look for a cloth or something to wrap around my hand when we collided."

She laughed and covered her mouth. "I'm so sorry – I'm such a klutz sometimes. Let me get a handkerchief out of my purse – I always carry one." Within moments she'd tied the blue floral hanky neatly around the nicks on his hand. The blood had dried by then, the pain subsiding to a dull throb, and he was grateful it hadn't been a deep wound.

He finished changing the tire and they climbed into the cab. "Let's go," she said, caressing his cheek.

Warmth flooded through him. He turned on the radio, settled back in his seat and checked his mirrors. "You constantly surprise me," he said as he pulled out into traffic.

"Really? I always thought I was entirely predictable." She laughed, and offered him a wry smile.

By the time they reached the picnic area, the shadows were long and there were only three cars in the parking lot. One of them was his parents' Lexus. Another was a red Mustang. "Uh-oh." He glanced at Gwen. "Chantelle's here."

"What? Why would she be here? Isn't it a *family* picnic?"

He nodded. "Yes. As to why she's here ... to cause trouble, most likely." He got out, hurried around to open Gwen's door, then held her hand as she stepped out. She was still covered in dirt and grime and there were even a few bloody scrapes on her knees. Likely he looked just as bad if not worse. At least they had a good reason for missing the event – Mom couldn't fault him for that.

They walked together hand-in-hand to where stragglers were folding picnic rugs and putting away Tupperware containers. "Mom, Dad," he called.

They turned to face the couple, his mother with her hands on her hips, his father crossing his arms. Chantelle stood behind them, her eyes narrowed. "Heath, there you are," Dad replied. "Hello, Gwen."

"Sorry we're late. We had a flat tire and it took longer than I thought to change it. I even cut my hand." He held it up.

"Oh dear, are you hurt?" Mom hurried to his side to examine the hand. "My darling boy."

"Where's Nana?" asked Heath.

Mom dropped his hand and her eyes clouded. "Uncle Braden took her home. She wasn't feeling well."

"Oh, I'm sorry to hear that. I hope she'll be okay. I'll give her a call later."

His mother nodded curtly. "Yes, that would be nice."

He noticed his father hadn't said another word, just watched him through darkened eyes with his arms still folded. "Mom, is something wrong?"

She sniffed, then straightened her back. "Yes, dear, something is very wrong. Chantelle has told us something quite disturbing ... I hope it's not true, but she assures us it is."

He made a show of rolling his eyes. "I can only imagine." Gwen squeezed his good hand.

"She says that you and Gwen aren't really engaged at all. That you only pretended so you could get your father's job. Is that right?"

Heath's stomach churned, and for a moment he considered continuing the lie. But he found he couldn't. "Mom, Dad ... I'm sorry. You're always pressuring me to settle down, get married. And Dad, you knew I was qualified to run the company, but you kept jerking it away. I didn't think it was fair ..."

"That's enough!" Dad shouted clenching his fists at his sides. "Don't make excuses. I didn't raise you to behave this way. Heck, I'm not sure who you are now."

"Don't say that, Dad. I feel bad about this – it was a spur of the moment decision and I shouldn't have done it ..."

Gwen stepped forward, her hands raised in surrender. "It was my fault, Mr. and Mrs. Montgomery – don't blame Heath. I needed the money and he offered to help me."

But Heath drew her back. "No, Gwen – the idea was mine, and the decision to prolong it was mine."

"Never mind," Mom insisted. "What's done is done. I suppose that's the end of the engagement-party planning. Nana was very disappointed to hear all her hard work was for nothing. I will speak with you later, Heath." She marched toward the parking lot with Dad following.

Chantelle closed in, a smirk on her painted lips. "Sorry about that, Heath, but ..."

"No, you're not," Heath interrupted. "You're not sorry at all. I don't know why you feel the need to nose into my family's business, but I feel sorry for you if you're really that desperate for attention."

"And thank you for saving us the trouble of letting everyone know, Chantelle," Gwen added. "We came here today to end the ruse, and now we don't have to."

Chantelle's face clouded over. "Oh ... you're welcome." She nodded numbly and walked back to her convertible.

Heath's face flamed and his gut churned. How dare she? It wasn't her place to say those things. Yes, he'd been wrong to lie, but that was on him. She was just trying to cause trouble – and she'd succeeded.

Within a minute, all of the remaining cars were gone, leaving his truck alone. Heath faced Gwen with a frown. "I'm sorry about that."

She shivered and rubbed her arms. "Please take me home."

HEATH CLICKED his tongue and the black gelding shot forward at a canter. He inhaled, letting the brisk morning air fill his lungs. It felt good to be outdoors, enjoying the sunrise and looking over the ranch.

After everything that had happened the day before, he needed today to himself. The ranch hands had the day off every Sunday, and he often spent the day at church and out riding. It was a time for him to get away from it all, to spend time thinking, praying and dreaming of what might be. But right now all he wanted to do was block out everything. Every time he let it, his mind wandered back to the day before – to Gwen, that kiss and the confrontation at the picnic area.

He shook his head and dug his heels into the gelding's sides. The animal pushed into a gallop, and he leaned forward over the horse's neck as the grass swept by beneath its flying hooves. *God, forgive me for lying and hurting my family ... and hurting Gwen,* he prayed. *Help me see a way forward ...*

Gradually the animal's pace slowed, finally stopping beside a narrow creek that bubbled and played over smooth rocks and around muddy bends. The horse dropped his head to drink, and Heath dismounted to stretch his legs. He walked into a thicket of hemlock and sat with his back against a tree trunk. The bark scratched through his shirt and he squinted up into the sky.

What should he do now?

A mewling caught his ear and he stood quickly, striding purposefully toward the noise. His gelding grazed nearby and the noise of the creek made it difficult to hear, but there it was again, a clear cry of distress.

He found the foal easily – it had mired itself in some thick mud by the creek's edge. He headed toward it, being careful to stay on solid ground. When he reached it, he could see it had been there a while – white foam flecked its mouth, its eyes were rolled back in its head and it struggled to pull its hooves free. "Shh, shhh ... I'm not gonna hurt you," he whispered, gently stroking its soft neck. "Now what have you gotten yourself into?"

He felt along each spindly leg ... no breaks as far

as he could tell. It had just gotten stuck. He worked gaps around the animal's legs with his fingers, then carefully pulled each leg out. Finally, the foal jerked backward and trotted off over the dry ground and out of reach.

He smiled and sat back on the ground to watch it go. It always felt good to set a creature free, to help alleviate its pain. That's why it had been so difficult with Gwen. He'd set her free, and even though he hated to do it, she'd thank him for it one day, he was sure. He wasn't ready to be the kind of man she wanted, was he? Did she even want him? She'd been so angry yesterday, then the kiss had turned everything upside down, and ... he wasn't sure what he felt.

He sighed and stood, brushing the dirt and mud from his jeans. He shook his head when he realized there was more mud on his hands than his jeans and he was only making things worse. Is that what he'd done, made everything worse? It certainly felt that way. Every time he'd made a choice, it only complicated his relationship with Gwen, with his parents, with Nana. Now he had what he'd set out for – the CEO position at Montgomery Ranches – and it was ashes in his mouth.

And on top of it all, he missed her. It had only been one day, but the way they'd left things, he wasn't sure if he'd see her again. They'd planned on breaking up, but never went through with it – quite the opposite if that kiss was any indicator. Still, it felt as though when he dropped her home, it was over. She hadn't met his eyes, just said goodbye and walked into her building without a backward glance.

The idea of not having Gwen in his life was too

much. His throat tightened and he gazed up at the sky overhead, watching the sunrise disappear, replaced by a clear blue. A memory of their shared kiss made his skin warm.

Heath returned to the gelding, remounted and spurred him toward the ranch house. He had a busy day ahead. And he had to think on what to do about Gwen, since he couldn't get her out of his head. Could they make it work? He wasn't sure, but there was only one way to find out.

"So THE POLICE have wrapped up their investigation." Adam sat in front of Heath's desk late Monday afternoon with a smile. "They arrested Paula Weston at home this morning, her and her husband. Apparently he was involved somehow."

Heath nodded. "Okay, great. So what do we have to do now?"

"Nothing yet. The prosecutor wants to meet with us later this week to talk through their case, but I don't think it's going to trial anytime soon. They'll talk to us about where the money is and hopefully let us know the chances of recovering it."

"Do we know how she managed it yet?"

"She was hiding the fraud under capital improvements." Adam leaned back in his chair. "Anyway, we'll know more after the meeting."

"Thanks for taking care of this. I really appreciate it – I've been ... distracted lately."

Adam grinned. "Yeah, I know – with Gwen, right? How's the fake engagement going?"

Heath sighed. "It's over."

"Yeah? That's a shame, I thought the two of you really had something there." He chuckled and linked his hands behind his head.

"Actually ..."

Adam's eyes widened. "Ohhhh ... you fell for her, didn't you? Oh, that is classic."

"I don't know what to do. We broke up, or meant to ... it's complicated. Chantelle showed up to this family picnic on Saturday and told them all about what was going on, thinking she could use it to win me back."

"No way!"

"Yes, she did; and no, she's not winning me back." Heath ran a hand through his hair and sighed. "Mom isn't speaking to me. Nana went home feeling unwell and won't answer the phone. Dad is the only one talking to me, and he's just avoiding the topic altogether, which beats the alternative."

"Well, good luck with all that." Adam stood, stretched and yawned. "I'm heading home for the day. It's been a long one."

"See you tomorrow." Heath rubbed his face as Adam left. He was glad the police had finished their investigation. He felt as though he'd handled that well, if nothing else. Tomorrow he would update Dad and the board on the issue. What he really wanted to do right now, though, was call Gwen and tell her about it. He pulled out his phone and stared at it. He'd only known her for a few weeks, but every time something good happened in his life, or even something bad, she was the one he wanted to talk to about it.

But given how they'd left things, a call wasn't good enough.

GWEN PUT IN HER EARBUDS, stood and stretched one arm over her head, then the other. She took off at a jog, her feet hitting the pavement in rhythm with the music. The park was familiar territory – she often jogged there. The sidewalk snaked its way through green fields, and junipers and hemlocks dotted the hills on either side.

It was time she got out of the house other than to go to work. For the past few weeks, she'd been caught up in Heath Montgomery's drama, but that had come to a crashing halt. Well, now was *her* time. She was not going to sit at home, watch TV on the couch, order take-out and go to bed early every night. She'd done enough moping after Edward left – she was all moped out.

She frowned and ran harder. She was upset, but why? After the divorce, she'd been relieved, angry, afraid, so many other emotions. But this felt different – like there was a hole in her chest that hadn't been there before. She'd almost called him this afternoon, but then remembered the look on his face when his mother told him she knew about their farce and she stopped herself. She didn't belong with him, certainly didn't fit in his family. And even if she had, they'd never accept her now. The deception was too much, she knew that.

Her feet pounded the pavement and sweat beaded on her forehead and ran down her cheeks. She just wanted to forget it all – her marriage, the divorce, poverty, Heath, everything. But memories still flashed across her mind's eye, ending with Heath's smiling face, his stubbled cheeks dimpling and his blue eyes sparkling.

God, help me to heal, she prayed. *Give me wisdom to move on.*

Her breathing was labored as she pushed herself up one more hill. At the top she stopped and rested her hands on her thighs to catch her breath. There was nothing she could do about it. If Heath wanted to move on and forget all about her, she couldn't stop him – and didn't have the strength left to try. She might as well do the same.

That resolve lasted until she approached her apartment and spotted a weather-worn blue pickup truck. Heath was leaning against the side of it truck, booted feet crossed at the ankles. He was dressed for work – dark suit, light blue shirt, power tie. He must have come straight from the office.

She slowed to a walk, hands on her hips. Sweat dripped off her face, which no doubt was currently red as a tomato, and soaked her tank top. Her hair hung in lank strands and she likely smelled like a gym locker room. Just great. "Hi," she said, stopping in front of him.

He smiled. "Hi."

"I wasn't expecting to see you."

His lips pursed. "I know. I just wanted to tell you something and I didn't want to wait, so I just thought I'd stop by. Is that okay?"

She nodded. "Sure, what is it?"

He ran a hand over his mouth and took a step

closer. "I talked to my brother about your ex and the alimony situation."

"Oh yeah. Thanks for doing that."

"Sure. Anyway, he looked into it and found the divorce settlement was already lopsided in your ex's favor, so even if he wants to contest, his chances at alimony are zero. He also says if you want to go back to court, he can overturn it and get you a better settlement."

"Wow. That's amazing."

"I hope it'll help."

"Well, it's good to know." She didn't really want to go back before a judge. She wanted to embrace Heath – her arms ached to – but she was covered in sweat.

Silence descended between them. She hugged herself tight to try and block out the awkwardness. He sighed and stepped closer, his eyes full of an intensity that brought heat to her cheeks. His hands dropped to his sides, clenching and unclenching as if he longed to reach out for her the same way she did for him. "Gwen ... are you free for dinner Saturday night?"

She blinked. "Dinner ... Saturday? Yes, I'm free."

"Great. I'll pick you up at 9 a.m."

Her brow furrowed. "9 a.m. for dinner?"

"Yeah. Is that okay?"

She shrugged. "It's Saturday and I don't have anything planned. I guess it's fine."

He grinned and nodded. "Great – I'll see you then. Oh, and pack an overnight bag."

"What?" Her pulse raced despite her confusion. "I'm not that kind of girl, Mr. Montgomery."

He threw his head back and laughed, sending shivers up her spine and making her smile. "I know.

It's not like that. Don't worry – there will be plenty of chaperones."

She frowned. "Okay, but what kind of clothes should I bring?"

"Something nice." He winked.

She set her hands on her hips. "Great, thanks. You're a lot of help."

He chuckled. "You'd look good in a feed sack." He walked around the truck and climbed in, waving to her out the window. "See you Saturday!"

Gwen waved goodbye, then turned to run into the apartment building, her thoughts in a whirl. An overnight bag? Where was he taking her? Excitement buzzed in her stomach as she climbed the stairs, and a smile drifted across her face. His drama might be the death of her, but she was still looking forward to Saturday.

15

GWEN CLOSED THE ZIPPER ON HER LUGGAGE AND catalogued all the contents in her mind. Had she packed everything she'd need? But how could she know, since Heath hadn't told her where they were going? She chewed on a fingernail, then pulled it from her mouth with a grimace when she realized she'd nibbled it down to the quick.

She glanced at her outfit – was it suitable? Again, who knew? She'd decided on the sea-blue dress with the spaghetti straps from the Montgomery wedding. Heath said it brought out her eyes, and she liked the way its hemline fell, soft and subtle, around her knees. Still, it felt odd to be so dressed up at 8:55 in the morning. Perhaps she should change ...

"Where are you going again?" called Diana from the kitchen.

"I don't know. He just said to pack for overnight. So I won't be back until ... well, I don't know. It better be by Monday morning, or Lisa will have my head."

"Well, just keep me updated so I know when to call the police." Diana chuckled and stirred the scrambled eggs. The toaster popped up two slices of toast.

Gwen's stomach churned, for reasons having nothing to do with food. "I'll call you when we get to ... our destination."

"Thanks!"

There was a knock at the door and Gwen hurried to answer it. Heath stood there in khakis, a button-down shirt and the ever-present cowboy boots. His dark hair was still damp and freshly combed. "Hi," he said with a wide smile.

"Hi," she replied quietly, mirroring their conversation from Monday. She felt like a nervous schoolgirl around him, which was ridiculous. She should pull herself together or he'd think she was a total ditz.

He leaned forward and kissed her softly, sending her heart into overdrive. "Good to see you," he whispered against her hair. "You look beautiful."

What was going on? Hadn't they ended things? She was utterly confused. She stepped back, her cheeks flaming. "We're off, Diana," she called tremulously. "See you soon."

Heath picked up Gwen's bag and led her out the door. A long black limousine waited by the curb, its engine idling. He handed her luggage to the driver, then opened the rear door for her. She slid in and smoothed her dress over her legs. "So are you going to tell me where we're headed yet?"

Heath chuckled. "Nope. You'll have to wait and see."

The limo pulled away from the curb and they chatted quietly. They leaned toward each other, closing the gap between them until his arm was around her shoulders, hugging her close. It was as natural as breathing, and the best place in the world to be.

They were so deep in conversation that when the car pulled to a stop she hadn't noticed their surroundings. The driver opened her door and she stepped outside to find she was at the jet center. The Montgomery jet was parked inside, waiting for them to board. She grinned and threw her arms around Heath's neck. "We're flying somewhere?"

He nodded, and she kissed him full on the mouth. His lips invited hers in and he held her there, feet suspended above the ground, while their souls entwined and her heart sang. If this was what a breakup was supposed to feel like, she'd take it.

Finally, he set her down with a smile. "Yes, we're flying."

"Okay." She scampered on board, unable to wipe the smile from her face. The last time she'd boarded that jet, she'd been heading into the unknown too – the destination was clear, but she didn't know Heath or what the weekend would bring. Her heart had been heavy over her own circumstances and she'd wondered if she'd ever feel hope again. This was different – she'd determined over the last five days to enjoy this, regardless of where it led. And if it led nowhere ... well, at least she'd have fun.

Heath took a seat and Gwen sidled next to him, linking her fingers through his. He smiled, talked about his week and asked about hers. She could imagine a future together, a life shared. For the first time in as long as she could remember, hope surged through her chest. But she knew that if it didn't happen, she could be content with that too.

GWEN SQUEEZED HEATH'S HAND. "Okay, we've been flying for five hours now, so you're going to have to cave and tell me where we're headed. Are you taking me to another country? Because I don't have a passport. If you want a girl to bring a passport on a date, you have to say so."

Heath raised her hand to study their entwined fingers. "No, we're not going overseas – that would take more than a weekend. I guess I can tell you since we'll be landing soon ... New York City."

"New York?" she squealed. "I've never been there before."

He laughed. "You'll love it."

Before long they'd landed at LaGuardia Airport and were in another sleek black limo, headed for Manhattan. Gwen leaned up against the window, eyes wide, straining to see as much of New York as she could.

Behind her, Heath chuckled at her enthusiasm and ran his fingers over her hand and arm. Each time he did, she glanced his way with a smile, her cheeks flushed with warmth. How had everything changed so much in such a short time? Only a week ago life had seemed so bleak – she didn't think she'd see Heath again, and couldn't imagine how they could make it work if she did. Now they were really together with no need to act, or pretend that their feelings were something they weren't. It was as though a veil had been lifted from her face, and she could see everything more clearly.

The car pulled up in front of a hotel that stretched skyward. She craned her neck to look up – the building covered an entire block with cool stone and acres of windows. An ornate *P* etched in glass shone above, and red carpets lined the stairs to the lobby. She climbed out of the car, taking Heath's offered hand, and together they ascended the stairs.

The hotel's decadence took her breath away. Everywhere she looked were wide staircases, gold-and-cream decor, shining tiles and plush carpets. "It's beautiful," she whispered. They checked in, each with their own room.

When Gwen opened the door to hers, she gasped in surprise. A huge bed with white bedspread sat by the window. A sitting area with thick rugs. Everything was decorated in the height of good taste. She took off her shoes and buried her toes in a rug, its thick wool tickling the soles of her feet. She grinned, then ran to the bed and leaped onto it with a cry of glee. Heath's room was right next door, and she wondered if he was doing the same thing.

No – this was all completely normal for him. But she usually stayed at a motel the rare times she'd gotten to travel (aside from camping with Ed). The Embassy Suites by the Seattle/Tacoma airport was the height of luxury she'd experienced until recently –

they'd offered free happy-hour cocktails and a breakfast buffet. This was on a whole different level – even
more impressive than the resort in Oregon.

She was tired after a long day of traveling – it felt
like forever since they'd left her apartment – and
Heath said to be ready to leave for dinner at 7 p.m.
She thought it a bit late for dinner, but wasn't going
to complain. She soaked in the tub for a half-hour,
read a magazine and ate a few of the chocolates from
the welcome basket at the end of her bed to tide
her over.

At seven, she was ready and waiting for Heath's
knock on the door, dressed in the red gown with the
plunging neckline. It was her favorite of the dresses
Heath had bought for her, since it was so unlike
anything she'd ever worn before. It attracted attention, something she'd never been comfortable with.
But with Heath she felt bold, strong, as though she
could handle anything life threw her way, including
attention.

He knocked and she hurried to open the door,
grabbing her clutch and a cream pashmina on the
way. She kissed him and he cupped her back with one
hand, stroking her cheek with the other. Her legs
quivered and she leaned against him, staring into his
eyes. "I feel like I've stepped into a movie," she said.

He laughed and took her hand. "I'm glad. You
deserve only the best."

Leading her to the elevators, he seemed almost
giddy, and his excitement was infectious. Who was
this new Heath, she wondered? He was usually so
withdrawn and solemn.

As they stepped outside, she saw tall trees and an

expansive green lawn across the street. "Oh, Central Park! Isn't it beautiful?"

He just nodded. "Let's take a look."

They crossed the road and strolled through the park hand in hand. She'd seen the park many times in movies, but never in person. It was so much more beautiful than she'd imagined: green grass in every direction, tall trees rising from the ground, leaves waving gently in the cool breeze. The sun had set behind the skyscrapers, casting long shadows. And people walked, ran and rode along the wide paths that wound in every direction.

Up ahead she spotted a line of carriages, their horses standing patiently, dashing drivers seated on top. Heath tugged her hand. "Let's take a ride."

Her eyes widened. "Really?"

"Sure, why not? It'll be fun." They climbed into an open carriage and Heath put his arm around her shoulders.

She slid next to him on the seat and let her gaze wander as they clip-clopped through the park. The cityscape as a backdrop and the gorgeous man at her side made her head spin. Thoughts whirled through her head — as wonderful as it was, what did it all mean? She sat up straight and faced Heath with a frown. "I'm having a great time. But can I ask you something?"

He raised an eyebrow. "Shoot."

"What's going on between us? I thought we'd broken up – or at least fake broken up. It seemed like the end, and I was ... well, pretty upset. Now this ... I mean, I'm not complaining, but ..." She sighed. "I guess I want to know what you're thinking."

He laughed, then kissed her softly. "I know – I thought we were doing the right thing by going our separate ways. But I missed you so much. I considered it all, and what I wanted from life, and I realized that what I wanted was you."

"Really?" She swallowed hard and her eyes stung with tears. "Well, I don't want to be without you either."

"That settles it, then. Let's stick together." He grinned and kissed her again, then added, "For real this time. But first, I just want to ask you something."

Gwen smiled. "Okay."

"My faith has become really important to me. I guess I'd like to know just where you stand."

Her cheeks flushed with warmth. "I love God. I always have. While I was married, I really struggled to attend church or spend time with God. Ed didn't like it — he thought it was a sign of weakness." She shook her head. "But now... I want to get back to spending time with God and with others who love Him the way I do."

He nodded, seeming satisfied with her response. Gwen leaned back against him, her gaze roving over the park. People walked, jogged and rode by, and Gwen's heart soared.

From then on, they talked about life and love and their hopes for the future. And when Heath kissed Gwen beneath a giant magnolia tree, she forgot about everything else.

∾

HEATH ROLLED ONTO HIS BACK, yawned and stretched

his arms high in the air. He hadn't slept so well in months. The bed was comfortable, the room was dark with plush curtains pulled across the windows.

Most of all, his heart was full. The previous evening had been everything he'd hoped it would. He and Gwen had toured Central Park in a horse-drawn carriage, dined at one of the trendiest restaurants in the city, and walked together back to the hotel. He only wished they didn't have to say goodbye in the hall outside their rooms. There were no more doubts in his mind. Now that he'd let Gwen into his heart, he didn't want to look back. He knew it was right where she was supposed to be and he couldn't be happier about his decision.

He smiled and hurried to shower, having slept later than he'd planned. Once he was dressed, he knocked on Gwen's door. She didn't take long to open it, already dressed in a long, flowing skirt and white blouse, her hair loose around her shoulders and her blue eyes gleamed. "Good morning," she said brightly.

He put his arms around her waist, pulled her close and kissed her softly. "Good morning." She giggled and returned his kiss, making his heart race. "Ready for breakfast?"

She nodded and pulled the door shut behind her. "Let's go."

They held hands as they walked, and Heath studied Gwen out of the corner of his eye. She seemed happy. Until last night he hadn't been certain she felt the same way about him as he did about her. Her smile warmed him all over. He'd never felt this way before about anyone, never come close to getting serious, having never found the right woman. He'd been waiting for that feeling, the certainty that now filled his heart.

In the restaurant downstairs, they sat across from each other as the mouth-watering aroma of pancakes, waffles, eggs and bacon filled the air around them. His stomach growled as a server poured them each a cup of coffee. "So what would you like to do today?" he asked.

She raised an eyebrow as she sipped at the coffee. "Hmmm ... you don't have anything planned?"

He shook his head. "No. We can do whatever you'd like. We have to head back to Montana this afternoon – the jet is booked for another flight in the morning and we both have work tomorrow. Other than that, we don't have any commitments."

Gwen stared out the nearby window at the tall buildings. There was always something exciting about New York City. Every time he'd been there, he always felt a surge of energy.

"I know it's corny and touristy, but I've always wanted to go to the top of the Empire State Building," she said with a grin.

He laughed. "Not corny at all. We can definitely do that."

"And I've heard Chinatown is amazing – maybe we could have lunch there."

"Do you mind walking?"

With a shake of her head, she slid one foot out from beneath the table. "Not at all – I even put on flats in the hope we'd do just that. I'd love to spend the day wandering around the city."

He took her hand and squeezed it. "That sounds perfect."

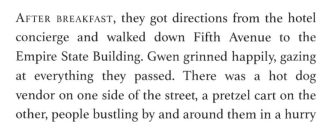

AFTER BREAKFAST, they got directions from the hotel concierge and walked down Fifth Avenue to the Empire State Building. Gwen grinned happily, gazing at everything they passed. There was a hot dog vendor on one side of the street, a pretzel cart on the other, people bustling by and around them in a hurry to get to wherever they were going, and yellow cabs stopping and starting by every curb.

Before long they could see the building, reaching up ahead of them with its telltale spike seeming to split the sky in two. It was just like *An Affair to Remember* – so romantic – and her nerves buzzed with excitement. Even more so when they reached the skyscraper's front doors, and Heath spun her toward him, cupped her cheeks in his hands and kissed her passionately. It took a moment to respond – he literally took her breath away. "What was that for?"

"Oh, just because." He grinned, and his eyes sparked with passion.

She couldn't help laughing at him. "I feel like I don't know you at all – you're so different from how you were."

He stroked her cheek. "I haven't changed. You've just cracked me out of my shell."

Her eyes widened and she kissed him back.

When they reached the observation deck, she walked cautiously to the windows and peered over. It was a long way down, and her head spun a little as she saw the streets filled with tiny people scurrying this way and that and toy cars inching forward. "This is amazing," she whispered.

Heath walked around the entire deck while she stood there pressed against the Plexiglas, then stopped beside her and took her hand, pulling her to him. She faced him with a smile. "What ...?" Then she froze as he dropped to one knee and pulled a small box from his pocket. He flipped it open and she saw an enormous pink diamond on a thin gold band, surrounded by white diamonds on both sides. "What are you ...?"

Heath grinned nervously. "I know it's corny and cheesy and we've already broken all the rules, but Gwen Alder, since the moment I saw you in the Lucky Diner, with your hair pulled back in a ponytail and wearing that stained apron, I just knew you were the one for me."

She laughed and hid her face behind her free hand, her heart racing. This couldn't be happening!

"We've already been engaged, but I don't think we did it quite right." He winked. "So my beautiful, sweet, thoughtful, *feisty* Gwen – will you do me the honor of marrying me? For real this time?"

She nodded, unable to speak, as tears began to trail down her cheeks. Around them, scattered applause broke through their bubble of joy and she smiled, embarrassed, as Heath stood and slid the ring onto her finger.

Gwen stared at it a moment, unable to believe it was all really happening. But when he took her into his arms and leaned her back to kiss her, she knew in her heart that she'd found the man who would comfort, protect and keep her always. He'd never leave her, never put his own needs before hers. She let herself drift away on the intensity and hope of that kiss.

"Can everyone please quiet down for a minute?" Heath yelled across the spacious deck. His parents' house was bigger than his, yet somehow it seemed cramped. The annual family get-together was the perfect time for their announcement. Problem was, once his family started catching up with each other it was almost impossible to stop them. He frowned and waved his hands, hoping they'd all get the hint.

Conversations ceased long enough for each person to look his way in surprise. Several people sat in nearby chairs. Twinkling lights flicked on as the sun dropped behind the mountain ranges and shadows crept across the ranch. "What is it, dear boy?" asked Nana, her voice shaky.

He glanced at the door that led inside to the kitchen, his stomach churning. Gwen was waiting for his signal, and he had no idea how his family would take the news. Then he nodded and smiled in Nana's direction. "I have an announcement to make, and I wanted to do it with everyone here."

His mother cocked her head to one side, not quite smiling, her forehead creased. He knew she didn't like being out of the loop.

Gwen opened the door and walked quickly to Heath's side. He took her hand with a smile and kissed it. "A lot of you have already met Gwen," he began, noting a few people nodding. "Most of you heard that we broke up. Most of you, of course, also heard that we weren't really together in the first place." He saw Dad frown and moved on. "Well, given time to think it over, we wanted you all to be the first to know that we've worked things out. And we're engaged!"

The extended family broke into loud exclamations of congratulations, applause and confusion. Several came up to shake Gwen's hand and examine the ring. Heath stood by her side, an arm around her waist. He knew how intimidating his family could be, but she seemed to be doing just fine.

Finally his parents approached, and the rest of the family quieted again. "So you're engaged?" Dad asked, his eyes narrowed. "What's it about this time?"

Heath steeled himself. He'd deserved that. "This is about being in love and planning to spend the rest of our lives together. I know I hurt you with my lies, but this time it's real."

Dad glanced at Gwen. "Is this true, young lady?"

She nodded, her eyes glistening. "I feel terrible about everything that happened before. It broke my heart when I thought I wouldn't see Heath, or any of you, again. But yes, it's true – Heath flew me to New York on Saturday and proposed on Sunday. And this time he had a ring."

His mother's eyes widened. "You're really engaged?"

"Yes," Heath replied.

She cried out and clapped her hands. "I knew you two were meant for each other! Oh, I'm so happy for you both!"

His father held out his hand for Heath to shake. "Son, I'm real proud of you. You've done well as CEO so far, as I knew you would. You managed that fraud situation well – though I would've preferred you included me in your confidence – and now you're finally engaged. Congratulations to both of you."

Heath's throat tightened as he took his father's hand. "Thanks, Dad."

His father embraced him – a brief hug, but still he couldn't remember the last time that had happened. "You know what this means?"

Heath shook his head.

"It means that as soon as the two of you are hitched, your father and I are taking that world trip we've been talking about," Mom replied. "Look out, Europe!"

All four of them laughed. Heath's heart filled with warmth and he kissed his mother on the cheek as she embraced him lovingly.

Then Nana appeared at Heath's side. Her head only reached to his elbow, but she'd never failed to get his attention she wanted. "Well, you two led us on a merry chase. But congratulations, my dear boy. And Gwen, welcome to the family. Now that I'm in remission, we can really get those wedding plans underway."

Gwen's eyes widened. "That's wonderful news, Nana." She bent to kiss the older woman on one cheek.

"We're a crazy lot," added Heath, staring at Gwen. "But we're yours if you'll have us." The group burst into laughter.

Gwen laughed along with them. "I can't wait."

Heath squeezed her close, then leaned forward to kiss her. He felt the same – he'd been waiting so long for the woman of his dreams. And now that he'd found her, he was impatient for their life together to finally begin.

THE END

EXCERPT: MAKE-BELIEVE WEDDING

A hot fireman with southern charm, a jilted journalist and two competing newspaper families steeped in a decades old feud. Could a fake wedding finally bring the enmity to an end?

Molly Beluga was abandoned at the altar and has no intention of heading back there anytime soon. A serious journalist working for her family's newspaper, her only plan is to focus on her career and to train her new Labrador puppy, Daisy, to behave.

Tim Holden left the family newspaper business to become a fireman with the Atlanta Fire Department. Now thirty, he's grown tired of bouncing between short-term relationships and is beginning to think that settling down and having a family is never going to happen for him.

When a gas leak in Molly's building brings them together, sparks fly, but in all the wrong ways. She thinks he's an arrogant jerk, he sees an entitled brat. Can they overcome first impressions and find a way to use their friendship to foster peace between their feuding families?

Chapter One

Tim Holden slammed a gloved hand into the heavy bag. It rocked to the left. He hit it with his left fist and it swung to the right. He followed up with two left jabs and a right hook.

"You takin' out your frustrations, Lieutenant?" asked Grant, one eyebrow arched as he slid a gym bag into his locker.

Tim grunted and hit the bag again. "You on shift today?"

Grant nodded. "Yep, just clocking in now. You?"

Tim glanced at the wall. Beside the words *ATLANTA FIRE DEPARTMENT – STATION 16* hung a slightly askew metal clock. It was close to eight a.m. He'd completed a twenty-four hour shift, then worked out. It was time to head home. "I'm almost done. Just clearing out the cobwebs." He grinned.

Sirens sounded throughout the station. Tim cocked his head to one side, waiting for the call-out information. The radio squawked: "Possible gas leak reported to 911 operator by employee at the Georgia *Times* Building, 3624 Peachtree Road."

Tim untied his gloves and set them in the basket with the ragged pile of red-and-white boxing gloves they all shared. He hurried to his locker, took out a navy uniform and put it on, pulled on his yellow turnout pants and jacket and tugged on his boots. He was bathed in sweat from boxing and at the tail end of a long shift, but it didn't matter – he had a job to do, along with the twenty other men who either hadn't clocked out yet or had just arrived for their shift. They didn't talk about the call-out – they didn't need to. Every one of them knew what they had to do.

And since the shift manager hadn't arrived for a handover yet, Tim would have to ride with them.

"You drivin'?" shouted Grant, as he climbed into the passenger seat of Tower One, the station's ladder truck.

Tim slapped on his hat even as he ran for the driver's side. "Sure am. That okay with you?"

Grant grinned. "Of course. I'm always happy to have my life flash before my eyes."

Tim grinned and climbed into the driver's seat, slamming the door shut. He glanced in the side mirror, watching the rest of the crew load up in the cab behind him save for one in the rear. "I don't know what you're talking about. You're safer than a baby in a crib when I'm driving." He cranked the engine, waited for the man out front to give him the all-clear, then edged the truck forward.

The fire station fronted onto a narrow road and only experienced drivers were able to pull out in one turn – the others had to ride shotgun until they could make it. He leaned over the steering wheel and turned it quickly, sending the truck in a wide sweeping curve and onto the lane. He checked his side mirrors to make sure the length of the truck didn't scrape the fencing that ran along the right hand side.

"You make it look so easy," complained Grant, his hand tight on the grab handle above his head.

Tim turned the truck onto the main road as Grant flipped on the sirens and lights. "You'll get it soon enough. Just takes practice." They had to shout to be heard over the noise.

"Where are we headed?" yelled one of the men in the back of the cab.

"Georgia *Times* building," shouted Tim. Even as he said it, his stomach roiled. He knew the building well. His family owned the Atlanta *Chronicle*, and the Georgia *Times* was their main rival for both circulation and breaking stories. Both newspapers were family-owned and had vied for second place behind the Atlanta *Journal-Constitution* for years. Tim had opted out of the dynasty, preferring to forge his own path.

But his father and brother still ran the business his grandfather built and had a tense relationship with the Beluga family, owners of the Times. Maybe none of them would see him there today, if he was lucky. He didn't feel like a confrontation. All he wanted to do was finish this call-out, head back to the station for a shower and home to bed. It had been a long day and between car accidents, domestic disputes and arson, he'd had just about all the drama he could take.

He pulled the truck to a stop in front of the building and killed the engine and siren. Lights still flashing, he and Grant climbed out of the truck. Within minutes the crew had donned oxygen tanks, masks, helmets and gloves and were ready to head into the building.

Another fire truck was already there, parked across from them. He walked toward Chad, a lieutenant from Station 14, who stood beside the truck, a cell phone against his ear. Chad hung up and grinned at Tim. "Lieutenant Holden – good to see y'all here."

"How's it going? You figured it out already?"

Chad nodded. "Yeah, we found the leak and got people on the way to work on it, but we could really use your help clearing all the floors."

Tim scanned the outside of the building. A group of harried-looking businesspeople stood in clusters around the garden and across the street from the building. "Looks like they evacuated okay."

Chad grunted. "Just protocol, but we gotta make sure everyone's out."

"Got it. We'll get started on that now."

"Great. If you can do the bottom floors and move up, my guys have already started at the top and are working their way down. You should meet in the middle somewhere."

Tim walked back to his team, who were waiting for orders. He relayed the plan and they all set off toward the building's entrance.

Tim ran up the stairs two at a time, stopping at the door marked FLOOR 8 to catch his breath. When he opened the door, the gas smell wasn't as strong as it was in the stairwell, which was a good sign. He hadn't come across any wayward office workers yet – so far, everyone had evacuated as they were supposed to.

He marched across the office space, divided by cubicles into smaller pieces. Each desk was littered with papers, pens and half-eaten breakfasts. Laptops sat open and coats hung on the backs of chairs that had been pushed out in a hurry and left there. So far, so good.

A noise in the corner near a line of offices with tall

glass windows caught his attention – a shuffling sound, like papers being rifled. He hurried toward it, and as he rounded the corner he saw a woman at a desk, hunched over a laptop, typing frantically on the keyboard. She pushed a pair of round black glasses up the bridge of her button nose and resumed her typing. "Excuse me? Miss?"

She spun around in her chair and gasped. "Oh, hi. Sorry, I know I'm supposed to evacuate, but look ..." She waved toward the open expanse of office behind him. "No fire. So I'm safe. Thank you for checking."

He couldn't help looking her over – cute brown bun piled on top of her head, peaches-and-cream complexion, fashionable suit that hugged her neat curves. His brow furrowed. He really couldn't stand when people decided to ignore the rules and make their own, putting him and the rest of his crew in danger. "Miss, you can't be here. It's not a fire, it's a gas leak, and we're still working on resolving it. It's time for you to evacuate. Now!" He set his hands on his hips and waited for her to move.

She pushed her glasses up again and smiled.

"Oh, right, sorry. Gas leak, huh? Just my luck. Um ... tell you what. Give me ten minutes and I'll be out of your hair, I promise."

He rolled his eyes. Of all the ... "Sorry, Miss, I can't give you ten minutes. You've got to leave now. Everyone else in the building is already standing outside in the designated evacuation zones. That's where you should be as well. Is what you're doing so important you'd risk your life to finish it?"

Her head tipped to one side and she made a face. "Um ..."

He grunted. "Okay, fine. Is it so important you'd risk *mine*?"

Her finely shaped eyebrows arched high and her mouth fell open. "Uh ..." Her eyes darted to the laptop screen. "It's just that I have to finish this story. I'm on a deadline and if I don't get it done the *Chron* will scoop us again. I know you probably don't care about that, but it's a big deal. Trust me." She returned to typing.

Tim's eyes narrowed. She couldn't be serious – of all the entitled, selfish ... never mind. He reached her in two steps, picked her up by the waist, threw her over his shoulder and around the back of his neck in a fireman's hold, and jogged toward the exit.

She wriggled and cried out. "Hey, put me down! You can't do this! Okay, okay, I get it, you want me to evacuate. I'll evacuate, just let me down!"

"You had your chance," he replied. "Now quit your hollering – I'm not going to endanger my team for your article."

She huffed and went still. He grinned as he carried her down the stairs. Thank Heaven she didn't weigh much more than the backpacks he trained with. Before long he'd reached ground level and exited the building. He set her feet down on the grass. "Now stay!" he commanded.

She pushed her glasses back up again and glared at him. "I am not a dog!"

He chuckled and patted her on the head. "Good girl." Then he turned and ran back toward the ladder truck to check on the rest of the crew. He could feel her anger aimed at his retreating back, and grinned again – he had to admit, she'd looked mighty cute with her glasses half falling off and her eyes burning with rage. Maybe he had more issues than he'd realized if he found himself so attracted to a woman who obviously hated him. He sighed inwardly.

Grant stepped out of the truck, chugging a bottle of water.

"Hey," said Tim. "I heard over the radio that they fixed the gas leak. That right?"

Grant nodded, his sunglasses pushed up onto his forehead where they almost always sat. "Yep, it's done. They're doing safety checks now."

"Good to know."

"Hey, were you carrying a woman out of the building just now?"

Tim chuckled. "Yeah – she refused to evacuate."

Grant laughed, held the two-way radio up to his mouth and pressed the side button. "Hey, y'all, you'll never guess what Tim just did."

Fitz's voice crackled back to them over the airwaves. He and the rest of the crew were still clearing floors – they'd kept going up the stairs when Tim stopped on the eighth. "What's that?"

"He found a woman refusing to evacuate and carried her out over his shoulder."

"She hot?" Fitz replied. Tim shook his head with a laugh. Fitz had a one-track mind.

"Pretty cute," replied Grant, one eyebrow raised.

Tim heard Fitz and the other members of the crew laugh, whistle and howl. Tim took a quick breath, wishing they'd quiet down. He glanced over his shoulder and found the woman looking their way, her hands on her hips. "Hey, cut it out," he hissed, his cheeks blazing. "She can hear you."

He'd felt some satisfaction in carrying her out

after her lack of concern for her life and the life of his team, but he had no desire to humiliate her. Not to mention how well it'd go down if she or anyone there discovered he was a Holden. If they did, the chief would hear about it, and Tim knew full well he wouldn't approve. No matter how much fun it could be to occasionally tease members of the public when they deserved it, he never seemed to be able to convince the chief of that.

He shrugged and headed back toward the building. Time to go back up and continue clearing floors. They'd work until they were done, or were given the all-clear for the building to be occupied again. He wiped the sweat from his brow with his sleeve and got back to work.

Steaming, Molly Beluga crossed her arms and glared at the fire truck as it pulled away from the curb. How dare that arrogant fireman treat her as though she were a sack of flour! She had a good mind to report him, but from the snickers she'd heard when he deposited her unceremoniously in the grass, she figured no one would give a hoot. Everyone else seemed to find the whole situation hilarious. Well, not her!

The fire marshals waved them all back into the building, and she marched inside with her chin jutted out. She still had to get her story finished and off to her editor in time for the next day's print run. She glanced down at her watch – she'd missed the deadline by fifteen minutes. Maybe her editor would give her a break, considering they'd all been stuck outside the office twiddling their thumbs for the past two hours. And since her editor was also her sister.

She felt a jab in her ribs and spun around to find Vicky Simpson, her best friend and roommate, grinning at her. "What are you smiling about?" she snapped, and wished she hadn't.

Vicky just giggled. "I saw you being carried out of the building by a big strong fireman – or am I mistaken?"

Molly rolled her eyes. "You're not mistaken. Can you believe that guy?"

Vicky sighed dreamily, clutching her hands to her chest. "No, I sure can't."

"Oh come on!" cried Molly. "He manhandled me!"

Vicky's eyes glinted. "Yes, he did." She waggled her eyebrows.

Molly sighed. "I suppose it *was* kind of funny."

"It was hilarious – we were all trying so hard not to burst out laughing. You looked so mad!" Vicky giggled again.

She inhaled sharply, her stomach churning. Vicky was right, she shouldn't let one arrogant fireman ruin her day. She had work to do, and she needed to focus on that, else she'd never get it done in time — that is if she hadn't missed out already.

Once upstairs, Molly hurried to her desk and quickly finished the article. It was a breakout on the mayor's new initiative to combat homelessness – the kind of piece she lived to write. So much of her time was spent reporting on festivals, food, social events or gossip that she couldn't help getting excited over writing about something important. After a last check for spelling and grammar, she attached it to an e-mail and hit send.

She leaned back in her chair with a sigh of satisfaction, a half-smile playing around her lips. It was an hour late, but maybe Amanda would let it fly just this once ...

Her desk phone rang and she picked it up, holding it against her ear with her shoulder. "Hello?"

"Sugar Pie, it's Granddad."

She smiled and leaned back in her chair again. "How are you? Did you play golf today?"

He chuckled. "You know I did."

"Did you win?"

"Of course." He laughed. "How about you? Takin' the world by storm?"

She shrugged and inhaled sharply. "I just sent an article to Amanda, so we'll see."

"Ah well, those things matter. But not as much as you might think, darlin'."

She frowned. "What do you mean, Granddad?"

"Oh, nothin', Sugar Pie. I'm just an old man thinkin' back over his life."

"But you achieved so much. And you're still young, Granddad ..."

He grunted. "Now I *know* you're lyin'."

She laughed and twirled a pen between her fingers. "Come on, Granddad, you sound a little down. Is everything okay?" He paused, and the silence made her sit up straight. "Granddad?"

"Oh, it's nothin', honey. Just wishin' I could change some things in my past, that's all. I'm gettin' old, and I guess I don't like that there are unresolved issues and things unsaid. When you get to my age, these are the things you think about – not your achievements, but the relationships you lost."

Her brow furrowed. "Who are you talking about?" She'd never heard him speak that way before. She hoped he wasn't ill.

"You remember me talkin' about my time at the *Chron*?"

"Of course."

He sighed. "I just wish things had happened differently. Wallace Holden was my best friend, did you know that?"

Her eyes narrowed. "I knew you were friends ..."

"And I never had another friend like him. Not after things went bad ... never mind, I'm bein' sentimental, is all. Nothin' for you to worry about, Sugar Pie."

"Okay." But she did worry – she couldn't help it. Usually Granddad was so gruff and matter-of-fact. He wasn't introspective or nostalgic – it wasn't his way. "But you *are* all right, aren't you?"

He chuckled. "I'm fine, just fine. I'll let you get back to takin' over the world. Just make sure you come by and see me sometime soon, okay?"

She agreed to see him on the weekend, then hung up, her thoughts spinning. She'd have to talk to Dad about this, find out if there was anything else going on. Granddad had spoken of Wallace Holden before, but never so fondly – usually his name was followed by a string of cusswords.

Molly spun around in her chair, hands linked behind her head – and found Amanda staring at her from her glass-walled office. She gestured for Molly to come in while fiddling with her headset.

Amanda was thirty-six and felt entitled to boss her thirty-two-year-old sister around – at least that's how it always felt to Molly. Even when they were kids playing school, Amanda was always the teacher or the principal and Molly the student. If they played family, Amanda was the mother and Molly the baby. Now as adults, Amanda was still telling her what to do – though as the *Times'* news editor, she really was Molly's boss.

Molly stood and hurried into her sister's office. Surely Amanda wouldn't push back on the article – it was one of the best she'd ever written. She had to see that. A surge of pride welled up, giving her goose pimples, and she smiled warmly at her sister. Amanda indicated a seat, and she sat slowly, then leaned forward over Amanda's desk.

Amanda finished her call and smiled tightly. "Nice piece."

Molly grinned. "I thought you'd like it."

Amanda linked her fingers together and set them on the desk, her hazel eyes boring into Molly's blues. "I just skimmed it, but I can see it's good. Still, I can't run it – not tomorrow."

Molly's nostrils flared. "Why not?"

"You know why not – you missed the deadline. Deadlines exist for a reason, Molly. You know that better than anyone."

"We had that ridiculous fire drill …"

"It wasn't a drill – there was a gas leak. It could've been a very dangerous situation, but thankfully it's now contained."

Amanda constantly amazed Molly. At work she was all business. Molly sometimes wondered where she'd got it from, then remembered how their grand-father and now her father ran the paper. But why did she always have to make Molly feel like she was eight years old again and she'd taken her favorite dolly? She straightened up and did her best to feel her age. "I understand that, but whatever it was, it interrupted me in the final stages of the article. I would've made the deadline ..."

Amanda sighed and ran a hand through her hair. It fell perfectly in place around her face, accenting her high cheekbones. "Molly, I'm sorry, but I can't make an exception for you. Layout needed everything from me ten minutes ago. Everyone else got their pieces to me in time, even with the interruption. If I start showing you leniency, it'll upset everyone else in the office, or I'll have to give everyone the same flexibility. Then layout suffers, the printers suffer, everyone suffers ... do you understand?"

Molly nodded, her stomach in knots. All that work for nothing.

"We'll run it the next day," Amanda added, with a softer tone and a half smile.

Molly frowned. "Of course ... unless someone else breaks the story first."

Amanda nodded, already turning her attention to her computer screen "You should take the rest of the day off."

"What? No, I'm fine. I've got that other thing ..."

"It's not a request. You've been working too hard. Take the afternoon off. Go out, have some fun. It's all part of our innovation initiative. Apparently people are more innovative when they get time off to rest."

"Okay." Molly wandered back to her desk, feeling deflated.

Vicky peered over the gray fabric cubicle partition. "How'd it go?"

"I missed the deadline."

"Oh suck. I'm sorry – I know how hard you worked on it."

"Thanks. And guess what? Amanda's sending me home for the rest of the day. Hey, you should come too. We can play hooky together."

"It's a deal. Just give me an hour or so, and I'll meet you back here. I've got a few leads I have to chase up first." Vicky smiled.

"Perfect, that will give me a chance to wrap things up as well."

Keep reading...

EXCERPT: DALTON

COWBOYS & DEBUTANTES

Chapter One

Dalton Williams scanned the crowd packed into the arena. Wide eyes peered through fence rails, button-down checked shirts and blue jeans crammed the rows of stadium seating. Eager mouths chomped on burgers, hot dogs, corn dogs, fried pickles and cotton candy and exclaimed over the spectacle below. The glare of stadium lighting illuminated the entire arena with an eerie glow.

Dalton's gaze drifted to land on the cowboy sitting astride a bronco in the bucking chute. The man adjusted his seat, locked his gloved hand around the leather strap and nodded. Stuart "Buck" Handley was the man to beat. He'd won the National Bronc Riding Championship trophy five years in a row – something no one thought could be done.

But last season Dalton had won, against all odds, throwing the whole circuit into a spin. Dalton had ridden against Buck for years and never come close to beating him. But last season had been different – he'd been at the top of his game after years of focus, practice and strength training. His dream of winning the championship had finally come true. Pundits were certain it was the start of a new era, one with Dalton at the helm.

But when the circuit started up again after the summer break, he'd torn a rotator cuff at the first event of the year. Now Buck Handley was back in the lead.

Dalton watched the bronc jump out of the chute, bucking and twisting, its hindquarters almost vertical above its head, ears laid back against its neck. Buck held on tight, his body flexing with the movements of the animal, one hand high in the air.

The buzz of the eight-second timer rang out and the crowd erupted into cheering and catcalls. Dalton shook his head and spat in the dirt as the announcer went wild, his voice echoing loudly through the cool night air.

"You ridin' tonight?" asked a soft feminine voice behind him.

He turned and nodded. "Yup."

Carrie Finnick stood there, her torn denim short-shorts and knotted flannel shirt leaving little to the imagination. "I'll be cheerin' for you," she said, laying a perfectly manicured hand on his forearm.

He glanced at it, then smiled. "Thanks, Carrie. I sure do appreciate it. I'll need all the support I can get."

"Oh, you're gonna win for sure – everyone knows that," she drawled, letting her fingers trail softly down his arm. His skin goose-pimpled beneath her touch.

He cleared his throat. "Well, I don't know about that. Buck just had a good ride that'll be hard to beat. But I'll sure try." He hated to be rude, but he had no interest in Carrie. She followed the circuit whenever they were in Texas and had hit on him every season. He'd taken her out to dinner once after a breakup, but hadn't felt any kind of spark. Not being the kind of man to lead a woman on, he'd left it at that. But she didn't seem to take 'no' for an answer – not where he was concerned, anyway.

The truth was, he hadn't dated anyone seriously since Jodie left him back in Chattanooga. If he was honest with himself, he hadn't given anyone a chance. But there was no time to think about that now. His ride was coming up and he had to get his mind straight. "I'd better go get ready," he said, touching the brim of his hat with his fingertips and nodding in her direction.

"I'll be lookin' out for you," she called after him.

He strolled over to the bucking chute and surveyed the animals corralled behind it, ready to go. He got to pick the one he wanted to ride and by now knew them all pretty well. The red roan was a solid performer, but tended to travel in a straight line with a standard bucking style. If he wanted to beat Buck's score, he'd need a horse with more of a twist to its stride.

His eyes landed on a gray quarter horse named Benny. At first glance, Benny looked like a mild-mannered old boy, but he knew differently. He pointed to Benny, and the cowboy with the rope nodded in acknowledgement. That done, now he just had to focus, to concentrate on what he had to do.

A group of children ran past with a bucket of popcorn, spilling kernels on the muddy ground as they went. They laughed and chattered amongst themselves, excited that the rodeo was in town and they got to watch the cowboys, arguing about who would win and who would be thrown. Dalton remembered doing the same with his friends when he was a boy in Chattanooga. He'd loved the rodeo and never missed it if he could help it.

He'd always wanted to be one of the cowboys who got to ride the wildest broncos around, and when he started on the circuit it was all he could do to keep from pinching himself. He couldn't believe he could ride for a living and have people cheer for him, look up to him, admire him.

But lately, things had been different. Ever since Jodie called to tell him she was through waiting for him to come home and had fallen for someone else, the spark had gone out of everything. The rides, the crowds, the bright lights – none of it filled him with the same excitement any more.

Buck stepped through a gate nearby and brushed off his chaps with both hands, dust swirling around him in a soft cloud. He spotted Dalton and grinned. "How'd ya like that, huh?"

"Sure was a good ride, Buck. It'll be hard to beat."

Buck raised an eyebrow. "But you're gonna try, I bet."

Dalton chuckled. "I sure will."

Buck leaned back against the fence and crossed his ankles. "How's yer shoulder?"

Dalton lifted his arm and circled it around a few

times, stretching out his shoulder with a grimace. "It's been better."

"Well, good luck to ya."

"Thanks, Buck. You staying to watch?"

"Ya bet. Wouldn't miss it." Buck's eyes glinted and he tipped his hat. "Gotta watch ya lose, boy."

Dalton laughed and strode toward the chute where Benny awaited him. He and Buck always teased each other that way. But after each event was over, they were first and foremost friends and usually ended the night playing blackjack over glasses of coke, each balancing bags of ice on the various body parts that hurt the worst.

"You ready?" asked a cowboy in a black Cowboy hat.

Dalton nodded, his eyes focused on the gray in front of him. The horse stamped a foot and pranced as far sideways as he could within the confines of the fence palings, breath expelling from distended nostrils clouding the cool fall air. He'd done this so many times before, he knew what was coming, and Dalton saw the whites of his eyes as he snorted and shook his head.

With a deep breath, Dalton climbed the rails of the chute and swung a leg over the animal's shivering back. His heart pounded and adrenaline coursed through his veins, exaggerating every sensation. Colors seemed brighter, every sound was amplified and the rough inside of the glove covering his hand as he clenched tight to the leather strap scratched at his skin.

Time stood still.

Then the gate swung open, Benny leaped forward

and Dalton dug his heels into the horse's sides. Benny swung left and spun in a circle, his heels kicking high above his head. Dalton held on tight, leaning back and forth, rotating with the movements of the animal beneath him. The noise of the crowd cheering him on swelled in his consciousness.

Then the eight-second buzzer sounded. The loudspeakers declared that it was a good ride and Dalton released his breath in a huff of relief. But as he loosened his grip on the strap, Benny spooked and bucked harder than ever as he swiveled to the right, crashing against the railings of the arena fence.

Pain shot through Dalton's leg and he cried out, grabbing it as the horse galloped out from under him. He felt his head spin, and everything faded to black as he landed with a thud on the grass to the gasps of the crowd.

Keep reading...

ALSO BY VIVI HOLT

Make-Believe

Make-Believe Fiancé

Make-Believe Wedding

Make-Believe Honeymoon

Cowboys & Debutantes

Dalton

Eamon

Parker

Visit my website at www.viviholt.com for an updated list of my books

ABOUT THE AUTHOR

Vivi Holt was born in Australia. She grew up in the country, where she spent her youth riding horses at Pony Club, and adventuring through the fields and rivers around the farm. Her father was a builder, turned saddler, and her mother a nurse, who stayed home to raise their four children.

After graduating from a degree in International Relations, Vivi moved to Atlanta, Georgia to work for a year. It was there that she met her husband, and they were married three years later. She spent seven years living in Atlanta and travelled to various parts of the United States during that time, falling in love with the beauty of that immense country and the American people.

Vivi also studied for a Bachelor of Information Technology, and worked in the field ever since until becoming a full-time writer in 2016. She now lives in Brisbane, Australia with her husband and three small children. Married to a Baptist pastor, she is very active in her local church.

Follow Vivi Holt
www.viviholt.com
vivi@viviholt.com